D1374222

OXSPELL

GILLIAN RUBINSTEIN

SIMON & SCHUSTER BOOKS FOR YOUNG READERS

ALSO BY GILLIAN RUBINSTEIN

Galax-Arena
Skymaze
Beyond the Labyrinth
Space Demons

I WOULD LIKE TO THANK EVERYONE WHO HELPED WITH THE RESEARCH FOR THIS BOOK, IN PARTICULAR, MY HUSBAND, PHILIP; PHIL STOTT AND SIMON HIGGINS; AND STUDENTS OF MORPHETT VALE AND CHRISTIES BEACH HIGH SCHOOLS.

AGAIN I ACKNOWLEDGE THE SUPPORT DURING THE WRITING OF THIS BOOK OF THE LITERATURE BOARD OF THE AUSTRALIA COUNCIL.

THANKS ALSO TO HYLAND HOUSE PUBLISHING FOR THEIR KIND PERMISSION TO REPRINT THE DIAGRAM ON PAGE 47.

SIMON & SCHUSTER BOOKS FOR YOUNG READERS
An imprint of Simon & Schuster Children's Publishing Division
1230 Avenue of the Americas, New York, New York 10020
Copyright © 1994 by Gillian Rubinstein
Originally published in Australia in 1994 by Hyland House Publishing Pty. Limited.
First American Edition, 1996
SIMON & SCHUSTER BOOKS FOR YOUNG READERS is a trademark of Simon & Schuster.

Book design by Anahid Hamparian
The text for this book is set in 11-point Caxton
Printed and bound in the United States of America
10 9 8 7 6 5 4 3 2 1
Library of Congress Cataloging-in-Publication Data
Rubinstein, Gillian.
Foxspell / by Gillian Rubinstein.
p.   cm.
Summary: Twelve-year-old Tod's mystical links with a spirit, half man and half fox, and with the natural world surrounding his grandmother's house in the Australian countryside challenge his attempt to adjust to the real world.
ISBN 0-689-80602-7
[1. Foxes—Fiction. 2. Supernatural—Fiction. 3. Australia—Fiction. 4. Human-animal relationships—Fiction. 5. Family life-Australia—Fiction. 6. Grandmothers—Fiction.] I. Title.
PZ7.R83133Fo 1996
[Fic]—dc20 96-11824

This book is dedicated to my father,
Thomas Kenneth Hanson

Oh. Mus' Reynolds. Mus' Reynolds! If I knowed all was
inside your head, I'd know something wuth knowing.
RUDYARD KIPLING: "THE WINGED HATS,"
PUCK OF POOK'S HILL

And daun Russell the fox stirte up atones.
GEOFFREY CHAUCER: "THE NUN'S PRIEST'S TALE,"
CANTERBURY TALES

BEGINNING

The young fox trotted down the railway track, nose twitching, brush swinging. It was just before midnight, a clear starry night with no moon, cold enough for the fox's breath to go before him in a little cloud. Behind him the twin rails of the train track curved up the hill toward the tunnel, glimmering faintly. On his right a tangle of bushes—bottlebrush and melaleuca—choked by long grass, screened the council depot and the garbage dump that lay behind it. On the other side the ground fell away steeply to meet back gardens filled with trees. The houses beyond were dark and silent, though in one a dog stirred and barked, making the fox trot more swiftly. Below the houses the orange and white lights of the suburbs stretched out for miles, but behind the depot the bush lay black.

The fox squeezed through a hole under the cyclone fence that surrounded the dump. It was used by cats and he left a few russet hairs on the wire along with their black and tabby ones. He wrinkled up his nose at the rank catty smell. He'd used this way in several times since his mother had chased him and his brothers and sister away from the den under the rocks in the quarry. The young foxes, their carefree cub days almost forgotten, had scattered through the foothills, following the corridors made by railway tracks and power lines through the outer suburbs, in their search for food and a safe territory.

Though he did not know it, this fox was the last survivor

of the litter. Two had been killed by cars, crossing Sheriffs Hill Road, and the third, the only vixen, ate poisoned bait in Auburn Hills. The young fox, their brother, had remained closest to his birthplace, and he had only survived so far because the garbage dump had been a reliable source of food, and at the depot workmen threw leftovers in the bins outside the canteen.

This night the depot was silent, apparently deserted. It smelled of all sorts of things, some bad like humans, trucks, and cats, some good like food scraps, making his mouth water.

The fox was starving. He had missed out on catching a rabbit earlier, and it had been dry and cold for some days so there were no slugs or insects around.

He slipped behind a huge earth-moving machine and into the shadow of a council truck. Here he paused and sniffed the cold air, ears back, nose high. He was uneasy. The human smell was strong and fresh, a mixture of sweat and cigarette smoke that was vaguely familiar. An image flashed into his mind of a human with blond hair, carrying a gun with the barrel sawn off short.

Danger the image said to him. *Danger.* There should be no humans here at night. Every day he heard the roar of the car engines that meant the council workers were leaving. The depot stayed empty, apart from the prowling cats, until the same engines roared the following morning and it came to life again as the humans returned.

One night only he had met another fox there, a huge dog fox, much older and bigger than him. Their eyes had locked under the moonlight, until the younger fox looked away and dropped onto his belly. The old fox stalked across the concrete parking area, broke into a lope just before the fence, and leaped clear over it. Since then the young fox had always looked out for the other one, but had never seen him again. He felt as if he knew him, without knowing who he was. He felt a bond between them.

This night he looked around, but saw nothing and smelled nothing except the human smell. He hesitated, almost turned to go back under the fence again, but hunger gnawed at his stomach. He had to eat. He ran out from behind the cover of the vehicles, into the floodlit yard, toward the canteen.

He heard two things. One was a weird voice, a human voice, but mechanical and distorted, droning over his head, hurting his ears. Then he heard a sharp crack, a noise that filled him with a sense of doom. The crack came again. Something hit him as if he had run into a sharp branch. He was running, but he could not run anymore. His feet slipped away from him. Red began to cloud his eyes. He tried to yelp, but his throat was closing. He took one last breath and then his spirit ran on, and hurled itself back into the earth it came from.

ONE

Tod, in the old house just down the road from the depot, heard the noises in his dreams. Since his family had arrived at his grandma's from Sydney he'd been sleeping badly. The mattress was lumpy, and the outside full of strange noises that gave him the creeps. Two trees by his window rubbed against each other, creaking like distant voices, and he often heard the monotonous *boobook boobook* of a pair of owls calling to each other from the gully.

Then there were the trains that went past late at night and early in the morning and the bells from the level crossing. But his dreams weren't full of tree or owl or train noises this time. He dreamed of gunshots and a hurt animal's yelping, and a mechanical voice that went on and on. *You have violated a protected area. The police were called. Leave immediately.*

He woke up still tired, mouth dry. He got out of bed and went in search of water. When he turned on the tap in the laundry, the pipes banged and shook the house and the water came out brown and smelling of chlorine. Tod decided against drinking it, and instead went outside to the rainwater tank that stood, covered in creepers, against the back of the house.

It was very early, a gray, pearly South Australian winter

morning, and the earliness together with his tiredness made him feel grim in a curiously satisfying way. He felt adult and mature as he contemplated life. There were good times and bad times. He knew that much already, even if he was only twelve, two years younger than Charm and five years younger than Dallas. You just had to sit it out through the bad times because things always got better in the end.

He splashed icy cold water from the tank onto his face and was making a cup out of his hands to drink from when Grandma popped out of the back door with a bucket in her hand.

"Don't stand there like a stunned mullet, young man," she chirped. "Take these scraps up to the chooks for me."

Things always got better in the end, Tod repeated to himself as he obediently took the bucket. Didn't they?

He stumbled on the steep steps going up to the chook run, and the bucket slipped from his hand. He went down on top of it, bashing his shin on the rim. Slimy scraps of vegetables, eggshells, and orange peel all mixed up with tea leaves shot out over the steps. A sharp smell like puke hit his nostrils. He swore loudly.

The screen door snapped open. He was sure his grand-mother had been standing inside watching him. "Mind your language, my lad!" she yelled up at him. For an old woman her voice was amazingly loud. Weren't old women meant to be quiet and gentle with soft, creaky voices? And they were meant to live in retirement homes away from everyone else, and smell of lavender water and have blue rinses. Grandma dressed like a man in old moleskin trousers and work boots. She did all the work on her own house and land, and she had more energy than Charm and Dallas put together.

Now she came tramping up the steps grumbling and complaining at Tod. "Crikey, you're a clumsy one. Can't you do a simple thing like feeding the chooks without making a mess of it? Get that stuff back in the bucket."

"It stinks," Tod said.

"Nothing wrong with a bit of stink," Grandma said, scooping the scraps up with her hands and giving the bucket back to Tod. "And don't swear out here. I don't want the neighbors thinking I've got a pack of lowlifes staying with me from Sydney."

"I've heard you swear," he retorted.

"I'm allowed to! I'm an adult. I've earned my right to swear when I want to. You're just a kid. So no swearing out here, okay?"

She grinned at him, making him unsure. Sometimes he almost liked her; other times she scared him. It was hard to tell what she was thinking, but her shiny dark eyes seemed to see right through him. He wondered if she minded having the whole family descend on her. She probably hated it.

He took the bucket from her and went on up the steep backyard to the terraced area where the hens and ducks were kept. The four khaki Campbells, three females and a drake with a glossy green head, greeted him with loud quacks and, when he opened the door of the tumbledown run, they fell over each other in their rush to get out at their breakfast. They pecked at his legs and at the bucket, tilting their heads sideways to peer up at him with greedy little black eyes.

The white leghorns and the pair of ginger-colored bantams were more dignified. They strutted around the mob of ducks, making gentle cluckings in their throats and darting in to peck at scraps as Tod emptied the bucket out on the ground. Some bits fell on the ducks' backs, and the boldest hen, named May after Grandma's sister who lived on the Sunshine

Coast, stepped nimbly in to peck at them.

Tod went into the run, wrinkling up his nose at the moist smell. In the straw at the back the ducks had made a nest, and there were two large eggs in it. He collected four eggs from the boxes too, three hen's eggs and one little bantam's. The run was made out of a haphazard collection of bits of tin and chicken wire, and he had to be careful not to scratch his hands.

Grandma had warned him about snakes and spiders too, but Tod wasn't afraid of either. He thought snakes and spiders were interesting. He would love to see a snake. A snake would be a great pet. He wondered if Mum would let him keep one. He peered under some of the old pieces of wood, but there were no snakes there and no lethal redbacks, just a few little brown spiders that pretended to be dead.

When he came out of the run, he put the bucket down carefully and squatted on the ground. The grayness was disappearing as the early morning sun began to warm the hillside. Two magpies were warbling in the big gum tree. He watched the poultry scratch and sift through the scraps. It was interesting how they reacted to one another. The drake and the hen called May were always trying each other out. Sometimes May backed down, but more often it was the drake. When the drake gave way he made a big fuss of his three wives, chivying them off to some other part of the yard. If May backed off, she stalked away deliberately as if she had just thought of something important she had to do up the hill.

"You should have a rooster," he called to Grandma, who was stooped over the vegetable beds, pulling out a few weeds that had dared to grow there.

"Wassat?" she called back, straightening up.

"You should get May a husband, get a rooster."

"Too much bloody trouble," she replied, brushing the soil off her hands. And couldn't resist adding, "Like all bloody men!"

Tod pretended not to hear her, looking away past the house to the suburbs and the sea on the horizon. The house had a great view, he'd grant anyone that. But that was about all it had. It clung onto the side of the hill, so old and tumbledown it looked as if a strong wind would blow it off altogether. It was a dump, he thought. He was living in a dump with his grandmother, his sisters, his mother (way too many women). His father was on the other side of the world and the only other male around was a drake, who let himself be bossed about by an old chook called May.

"Don't just sit there dreaming, boy!" Grandma had started nagging again. "Come and give me a hand."

Tod was saved from having to answer by the bells at the level crossing, which began to ring insistently. The ground shook a little as a train went slowly up the hill above the yard. It looked as though it might wobble off the track and fall down on top of the chooks. Grandma called it a red hen, that old train. White hens squashed by a red hen, he thought and grinned to himself. He could pretend he hadn't heard Grandma through the noise. Stupid place to live, right on a train track. The freight trains woke him up in the middle of the night. You could hear them coming for about ten minutes, straining up the hill, hooting mournfully at every crossing. Then the ding dongs, as his mother called them, started going, and the house started to shake, and the huge train lumbered past. "You'll get used to it," Grandma said, but Tod didn't intend to stay long enough to get used to it. He thought of jumping on the train and riding it out of here, riding it all the way to Melbourne, and then another train, back to Sydney, back to life as it used to be.

Then the bad times would be over, and the good times back again, and he wouldn't have to go to the new school.

He rubbed his hand across his face and caught a faint whiff of food scraps and chicken manure. He got to his feet, picked up the bucket with the eggs, and went down the steps to the house. The train noise was fading. It must be nearly at the tunnel. He could hear Grandma now, saying, "Clean them eggs. Wipe them, now, don't wash them under the tap. And rinse the cloth out after."

"Okay, okay," Tod groaned, as he went into the house.

It had its own smell too—old house, old cats, and the homemade furniture polish Grandma made out of lemon juice and linseed oil. He could smell it now, lurking beneath the breakfast smells of toast and coffee and the scent from the bathroom of Charm's latest conditioner. His oldest sister, Dallas, was standing outside the bathroom door, a towel under one arm and a textbook under the other.

"Hurry up, Charm," she shouted. "You're not the only one that needs to get ready." She took a swig from the mug she somehow managed to hold between her two hands, hunching over to get at it, her face disappearing beneath her thick springy hair.

"Where's Mum?" Tod said.

"Still in bed," Dallas replied. "You want breakfast? I'll fix you something. Charm's probably going to be another two hours in there. She doesn't care if she's late for school or not. But I do care. So who gets first shower?"

Tod didn't even bother to answer that question. "I can help myself to breakfast," he mumbled.

"Nah, s'okay, I'll do it for you. Can't start a new school on an empty tummy!" She'd always babied him a bit; she liked the role of big sister. Dallas mothered everyone, even Mum. She put the towel and the book down on the kitchen table. Tod began to wipe the eggs. The carton in the fridge was full. He left the eggs on the draining board, and went through to the back of the house. The original back door opened into a long enclosed fiberboard lean-to, tacked onto the older stone house wall. One end of this was his room, tiny with louvre windows, the other the laundry and general junk area. Grandma saved everything. She was a recycler's dream. Two old wardrobes were stuffed full of newspapers and plastic bags, their drawers overflowing with bits of string and tin ties. The spare egg cartons were stored in a splintery tea chest with ancient stencils on its sides. Tod lifted one out, held it to his nose. There was the faintest smell of tea and cold cardboard.

"You want an egg?" Dallas had poured orange juice, and water was boiling on the green enamel stove. "They're definitely fresh!"

"Straight from the chook's bum," Tod said. "I think I'll skip the egg today." He lined the eggs up in the carton and went to put it in the fridge.

"Don't forget to put the date on," Dallas said. "Here, you want me to do it?"

"I can do it," Tod said. "I can write, you know." Dallas gave him a pencil and pretended not to watch.

"What is the date?" Tod said. "July the something or other?"

"August fifth."

"August? What happened to July?" He thought of all the things that had happened in the last couple of months. Dad deciding he had to go back to England to live. Mum losing her job at the same time. The move to Grandma's house in Adelaide, the place where Mum had grown up, where she still had friends who would help her get her new career going. He bit the inside of his lip, concentrating as he wrote on the box,

August 5th. He knew he'd got it right, because he felt Dallas relax.

He put the carton in the fridge and sat down at the table. The chairs were plastic seated and had chrome legs. When he sat down at the kitchen table in their house in Sydney, he used to feel hungry at once, but these chairs didn't make him feel hungry at all.

"Writing's easier than reading," he told Dallas. He didn't mind talking to her because he always felt she was on his side, unlike Charm and even Mum. Charm blamed him, called him stupid, and Mum blamed the system, said he'd never been taught properly. But Charm and Dallas had both learned to read, despite the system. Charm never read anything except magazines, but Dallas was really interested in books and reading and studying.

"Perhaps the new school will help," Dallas said, getting a bowl out of the cupboard. "D'you want some cereal?"

"What is there?"

"Just All-Bran, I think."

"Any bread? I'll have some toast." Dallas plugged in the old-fashioned toaster, and put in two slices of bread.

"It's not that I can't read," Tod said. "I can read the letters all right. I just don't see the point of all those words. And I'd rather be outside, doing things, you know?"

"Yeah, I know." Dallas came and sat down next to him. "But you need to be able to read well to study, and you need to study to get anywhere. That's what I think." She looked around the kitchen and a savage look came over her usually gentle face. "I'm never going to end up like this," she said quietly. "I will never, ever go back to my mother with three children. I'm going to be rich if it kills me."

"Something's burning," Tod interrupted.

"Oh no, it's the toast!" His sister leaped to her feet. "Look at it," she moaned, holding up the charred slices.

There was a scuffling sound from the laundry—Grandma taking off her boots. She came padding into the kitchen in her old slippers at the same time Charm burst in through the other door.

"For heaven's sake, Dallas," Charm shouted, "what the hell are you doing? Smells like a crematorium in here."

Grandma chuckled as though she'd scored some obscure point over someone. "You've gotta watch that toaster, Dallas. You've gotta be quick with that one! Never mind, the old chooks'll eat it. Charcoal's good for 'em."

"Make me a coffee, Dallas." Charm flung herself down next to Tod, and ran her fingers through her hair. It was black like Dallas's and Tod's, but whereas Tod's was straight and shiny, and Dallas's was thick and curly, Charm's hair looked as if it were made from some other material altogether, something gothic like cobwebs, and it had a greenish tinge, probably due to the fact that she had only recently dyed it back to its original color. It had been blond before that.

"Make it yourself," Dallas retorted. She'd given up mothering Charm years ago. "I'm going in the bathroom now."

"Selfish toad," Charm yelled after her as Dallas disappeared into the steam-filled bathroom. They heard water running and a few moments later a scream from Dallas. "You cow, you've taken all the hot water!"

"No more hot water till tomorrow," Grandma said with satisfaction. "It's only a small tank. Always used to be plenty for the whole family."

Charm buried her face in her hands. Through her fingers she mumbled, "Toddy, I bet you can make that antique toaster work. Make me some toast."

"Make it yourself, girl," snapped Grandma, who after only forty-eight hours reckoned she'd got Charm's number.

"I don't mind." Tod got up from the table. He took two more slices of bread from the packet.

"What's that terrible smell?" His mother came into the kitchen, wrapped in a rose-pink kimono with a silver dragon on the back. Her long black hair framed her pale face, making her look just like Morticia Addams. She sat down at the table. "Oh! I feel like hell. I've got a crick in my neck from that blasted couch."

"No one's forcing you to stay," Grandma said acidly. "Put the kettle on, Tod, there's a good lad."

"Put it on yourself, girl," Charm mimicked her voice exactly, and sent Tod a wicked look from under her eyebrows. He grinned as he filled the kettle with water and took the toast out at just the right moment so that it was golden brown. Charm could make him feel terrible, but when she was being nice, he liked her more than anyone else in the world.

Leonie, Tod's mother, sat with her head in her hands. There was a brief silence while Tod and Charm ate their toast. The kettle began to whistle. Grandma got up and made the tea.

"Here," she said, pushing a big, brown mug toward Leonie. "Drink this, it'll wake you up."

"Thanks, Ma. Have you got a ciggy too?"

"Mum," Charm said, "you've given it up, remember?"

"Not today, I haven't. In fact, I gave up giving up last night, if you want to know."

"You're hopeless," Charm told her. "You've got no willpower at all."

"Give me a break." Leonie groaned. "I don't need a lecture from my teenage daughter. I just need a fag. I'll give it up when we get settled, I promise. Where are they, Ma?"

"In the bag in my bedroom," Grandma said. "Toddy'll get 'em."

Grandma's bedroom was dim, blinds still down, bed unmade. The big black-and-white cat, Inkspot, was curled in a ball among the bedclothes. He opened an eye when Tod went toward the bed, saw it was a stranger, uncurled in one swift movement, and streaked out of the room. Tod was disappointed. He would have liked to have been Inkspot's friend. But the cat only trusted Grandma.

He looked around the room. There was a faint flowery smell, sweet and old, together with a smell of dust. There was plenty of dust on the old furniture, on the photo frames and the little pots and jars. He picked up a black-and-white picture of his grandfather at the beach, a young man with sleek black hair and an embarrassed grin. There was another photo of him as an older man, sitting on the ground with two Aboriginal men. All three were wearing stock hats. Next to the photos of Grandpa stood a faded color photo of his mother and her sister, Carol, when they were little. They were wearing shorts and matching tops and had white ribbons in their hair. Most of the other photos were of dogs that Grandma had owned through her life. He remembered the last of them, the kelpie cross with little golden patches above her eyes. The last time they'd visited Grandma when he was ten, she had been alive, but now she was dead.

It would be better with a dog here, he thought, and wondered if he could persuade Grandma to get a puppy. He was thinking about the puppy when he heard his mother shout from the kitchen.

"What are you up to in there, Tod?"

"I hope you're not prying into my things," Grandma yelled.

He remembered what he was looking for, found the bag, and took a packet of cigarettes out of it.

Back in the kitchen Grandma was grumbling at him. "Stay out of my things. I don't want anyone messing around in them."

"But you asked me to get the cigarettes," he protested.

Charm wagged a finger at him. *"You have violated a protected area."*

The words broke his dream. He remembered hearing them in the night. He remembered the gunshots, the yelping animal, and something else, a feeling of being part of the earth, of being made of earth, and a diving feeling, diving . . . not exactly into the earth but into some other place, some other world. He shivered.

Leonie lit a cigarette and dragged on it. The smell of smoke filled the kitchen. Dallas, who had returned dressed in school uniform, made an exaggerated face. Grandma lit up too. Dallas flapped the smoke away with her hand.

"You're not both going to smoke all the time, are you?" she wailed. "What about passive smoking? What about Charm's asthma?"

Charm put her hand to her chest and began coughing dramatically. "Help, help," she moaned. "I can't breathe." Then she recovered remarkably quickly.

"I don't get asthma anymore," she said. She pointed her finger at Leonie and intoned, *"Leave immediately."*

"What is that?" Leonie said. "I kept hearing it in the night. Is it some sort of alarm?"

"It's from the depot," Grandma said. "Some fancy new idea. They reckon it stops vandals. I guess they were up there last night again. Wonder how much damage they've done."

"What sort of things do they do?" Charm said.

"Oh, that graffiti stuff, try to get into the machines, break a few windows. All the usual mischief kids get up to." She peered at Tod through the smoke with narrowed eyes. "I hope he's not that sort, is he?" she said to Leonie.

"More likely to be Charm," Dallas muttered.

"Thanks," Charm replied, getting up swiftly. "I'm out of here. See you."

"Don't you want me to drive you down to school?" Leonie said.

"Mum, no way."

"You will go, won't you?" Leonie pleaded. "You promised you'd stop ditching when we left Sydney."

"I'll give it a try," Charm said and grinned her wicked grin. They heard her chanting down the passageway, *"You have violated a protected area. The police were called. Leave immediately."* Then the door slammed and she was gone.

"You're going to have trouble with that one," Grandma said.

Leonie immediately leaped to Charm's defense. "She's all right, really. It's just her age. She's wonderful compared with some of her friends."

Grandma snorted.

"She gives Mum great material for her stand-up routines," Dallas commented. "Sometimes I think she does it all just so you can be funny about her," she added to her mother.

Grandma snorted again. "And of all the half-cracked ideas to come up with, girl, that one takes the cake. Standing up in front of strangers making jokes about your family. You'd better not start being funny about me, I'm warning you."

"Oh, come on, Ma. If I can't be funny about you I lose all my best material." Leonie winked at Tod and Dallas.

"And what about this young man?" Grandma said, indicating Tod. "It's bad enough for him having to live in a houseful of women, without his mother standing up in the pub making jokes about tampons and condoms."

"He doesn't mind, do you, Toddy?" Leonie turned her huge dark eyes on him and looked at him soulfully. It was the same look she gave him when she asked him to do things for her and it worked every time.

"Not really," he said. "Not as long as my friends don't hear you. But I haven't got any friends here anyway, so I guess it doesn't matter." Then, because there was a silence that seemed to need to be filled, as if there was something they had forgotten to talk about properly, he added quietly, "I miss Dad though."

"We all miss him," Leonie said. "But it *won't* be long before he's back."

Grandma made a scoffing noise.

"He is coming back," Leonie continued determinedly, giving Grandma a challenging look.

"I'll believe it when I see him walk in that door," Grandma replied, stubbing out her cigarette in her saucer.

"He just needed some time off, away from the family," Leonie said. "He needed to go back to England and see his folks."

"Midlife crisis," Dallas explained, getting up. "I must dash."

"I'll drive you," Leonie offered, making no effort to move.

"I'll be late if I wait for you, Mum. I'll get the train."

"You'll have to run to make the 8:02," Grandma said. "Midlife crisis my eye! He ran out on you, girl, and you've got to face up to it."

Tod saw Dallas's face just before she left the room. She

looked miserable. His mother lit another cigarette with a swift, angry movement. He thought she and Grandma might be about to start a fight about Dad. He didn't want to hear it. Without saying anything he went to his room and got ready to go to school.

TWO

No one had said that about Dad running out on them before. Tod was still thinking about it as he let himself out of the front door of the house and went down the chipped concrete steps between the two huge evil-looking plants. They had long grayish leaves—if you could call such twisted, sword-shaped things leaves—with points as sharp as needles. They looked like houseplants that had gone berserk. They were bigger than he was. When he looked back they seemed to be guarding the house, but they didn't make him feel safe. They made him feel creepy.

There were two ways to walk to the school. He remembered that from their last visit to Adelaide two years before when he and Charm used to race each other down to the oval and play on the equipment. You could walk to the end of the road, cross the street, and walk straight into the school yard through the top gate, or you could turn the other way and go through a small reserve, with long grass and gum trees sloping away to a deep gully, take the next street and go into the school through the bottom gate.

Feeling he needed the extra time to think, Tod went this way. Had his father really run out on them, as Grandma had said? She'd said it with a note of triumph in her voice as though it was only what she'd expected. He realized with a shock of insight that she wasn't too keen on Dad. She went on and on about him being a Pom but even if he hadn't been British she still wouldn't have liked him. She thought he was a nutter, writing poetry and working for what she called dead-beat organizations and never having two cents to rub together.

So what she had said back at the house during breakfast needn't be true. It could be the sort of thing people said when they didn't like someone. They tried to make them out to be worse than they were. They twisted what they did to make it sound bad. That must be what Grandma was doing now. But why had Dad gone back to England? And why was he staying away for so long? And why when Tod asked his mother when his father would be back did she say, "I'm not quite sure"?

He tried to remember exactly what Dad had told them before he went. He wished he'd paid more attention. He hadn't really taken in all the discussions that went on. Suddenly it had all seemed settled—his father was getting the plane to England next week, tomorrow, this afternoon, now. . . .

Dad always missed his family in England, Tod knew that. He phoned them all the time, running up huge bills that threw Mum into despair. They'd lived in the city, in the middle of Sydney, because that was where all Mum's friends were, but his father had always described himself as a country boy. He took them out on drives to places like Camden and Windsor, especially in winter while everything was still green, and when they got out of the car he took deep breaths of the country air as though it were a life force that was going to save him.

Sometimes he hit himself on the chest and said he had a huge hollow space inside him that was homesickness for the landscape he grew up in.

"If I don't see it again, I think I'll die," Tod remembered him saying. And then his father grabbed a handful of flowers from a vase on the table and shook them in the children's faces. Water dripped on the floor as he shouted, "I'm like these bloody flowers. I'm cut off from everything, and there's nothing left to do but die."

And Tod remembered the faint smell of decay that already clung to the flower stems.

Once someone had returned to their own landscape did they ever come back again to the new one? He had no way of knowing. But between the hollowness and the cut flowers he was not sure they did.

His father's name was Laurie, short for Laurence. The children teased him about it, because he never learned to call trucks anything else but lorries, so they used to call him truck, or sometimes semi.

Truck, Tod said to himself, trying to summon up his father's presence, but there was nothing there, except the magpies calling in the reserve and the bells on the level crossing ringing as a train came slowly down the hill.

He stopped to watch it go by. No one was going to care at school if he was late on his first day. It was a passenger train, the Overland from Melbourne. Travelers looked out of the window. A couple of children waved at him, and he waved back. As the train rattled past he caught a flash of orangy brown between each carriage. It was something caught on the fence surrounding the depot. Once the train had gone, he crossed the track to have a closer look, remembering Grandma's remarks about vandals and the weird voice alarm in the night.

A dead animal was spread-eagle on the fence. Someone had tied it on with wire. At first he thought it was a large ginger cat, and then he saw its dog-shaped muzzle and ears. But it wasn't a dog. It had a long bushy tail, every shade of brownish red, white at the tip. He recognized it from TV. It was a fox.

Its eyes were half open and there was a small round hole in its head, from which blood had oozed. Someone had shot it. Tod looked around. The animal was hidden from the depot entrance by a row of shrubs. It could only be seen from the train track. He looked back at it. It filled him with sorrow seeing it strung up on the wire fence like that. He didn't know what to do about it. It was dead—there was nothing he could do for it—but he couldn't bear to leave it like that.

He reached up, untwisted the wire, and lifted the body down. It was already rigid, but the fur was soft. The black feet were small and neat. Inside the half-open mouth he could see sharp white teeth. He wished he could keep the dead fox but he knew enough about death to know that within a day it would start to stink. Still he wanted to do something for it, so he carried it down to the gully and buried it.

It wasn't a real grave—he had nothing to dig with, but the earth was soft enough down by the creek for him to burrow quite deeply with his hands. He covered the fox with dead leaves. Then he found some large stones in the creek bed, and made a sort of cairn above the leaves. Finally he picked some sprays of early-flowering wattle and draped them over the cairn.

He squatted down on his heels and thought about the fox. It was back in the earth again; it came from the earth and now it was back in it. Down among the bushes in the gully, his hands covered in dirt from digging the grave, mud on his shoes from the creek, he felt as if he belonged to the earth too. He wished he'd seen the fox alive. He would love to see a wild fox. Perhaps he'd go to the quarries and look for them there.

He wondered who had shot it. Shooting it wasn't so awful. It was stringing it up on the fence like that that outraged him. I'm sorry, he said to the fox's spirit, wherever it was. I'm sorry they did that to you.

Then he got up, wiped his hands on his jeans, and went down to the school.

He was late. There were no children outside in the school grounds. He crossed the road and followed the sign that said OFFICE. When he walked in his mother was in there talking to the secretary.

They both turned and looked at him.

"Here he is!" his mother said, acting bright and unconcerned. "Tod, this is Mrs. Crane."

Mrs. Crane looked tiny next to Leonie. She had short gray hair and wore big glasses. She sounded very cheerful as if she had decided years ago that working in a primary school was enormous fun and nothing was going to make her change her mind.

"Hello, dear," she said to Tod, twinkling at him through the big glasses. "We thought you'd got yourself lost. Mum tells me you're in year seven. You're going to be in Ms. Linkman's class. Do you want to walk over with him?" she said to Leonie. "It's down those steps and in through the second door. Room twelve at the end of the passage, opposite the resource center. I'd come down with you, but someone's got to hold the fort here."

"We'll find it, thanks very much." Leonie swept off grandly. As they went down the steps she said to Tod, "Where on earth did you go? You knew I wanted to come down with you. I've got your old books and all that stuff for your teacher."

"I forgot," Tod said. "I thought I'd better get to school. You didn't go with Charm and Dallas."

"They'd have assassinated me if I had," Leonie said. "Anyway, don't change the subject. Where were you? If you were in such a hurry to get to school how come you arrived after I did?"

Tod shrugged. "Must have taken the long way around." He didn't want to tell Mum about the fox. He didn't want to tell anyone. He decided it would be his secret. And then on the spot he decided he would find out who'd killed it and pay them back.

"Whatever are you thinking about, Toddy? You look positively ferocious. School's not going to be that bad, hon." Leonie took his arm as they went down the passageway but he managed to extricate himself before they entered the classroom.

He'd been in year six in Sydney. Funny to think he'd been promoted a whole year just by moving to another state. Of course, it was the same class really, the last year of primary school, just a different name. He looked around at the kids quickly before staring out of the window as if there was something really interesting outside. It was stupid to expect any familiar faces, but all the same it was a bit of a shock to see so many completely new people.

Some of them were looking at him, but most of the class were gazing in fascination at Leonie. Tod was so used to her he forgot how strange she looked to other people. She'd never looked strange in Surry Hills—everyone looked more or less like her there—but here she looked like a member of another species, not human at all. Her jet-black hair hung around her pale face, and she had made up her eyes so they looked even darker and huger than usual. She was wearing two skirts, a midlength black fringed one over a long peacock blue one, and she had strands of beads and two scarves in almost the same blue around her neck. Next to Ms. Linkman, who was compact and well-scrubbed like a netball player, she looked vaguely dirty but also glamorous, like a member of the Russian aristocracy shortly after the revolution.

Leonie always came alight when she had any sort of audience. Even if she spoke on the phone or walked into a shop to buy something her face and voice changed from their ordinary shape and tone to more exciting, more vivid versions. Tod watched it happen now, his heart sinking slightly. He loved his mother and was proud of her, but she could really embarrass him too. He just hoped she wouldn't launch into a full routine of her stage act. She was quite capable of it.

"Hi there," she said, putting her hand out briskly to Ms. Linkman. To Tod's horror she had assumed an American accent. What on earth was she going to say?

"This is my little guy, Toddy," Leonie went on, giving Ms. Linkman a nudge with her elbow that sent her spinning into the blackboard. "Kinda cute, ain't he? But don't be fooled by those innocent looks, no sirree. This kid's meaner than a cut snake effan you cross him. You wanna show these folks whut ya can do, Toddy?"

He backed away, shaking his head frantically at her.

"Oh, pulease," Leonie begged him, pursuing him. She had him trapped in a corner. "Black belt in karate," she hissed over her shoulder at the rows of faces. Tod could see disbelief and scorn spreading like chicken pox over them. Leonie grabbed him by the hand and at the same moment threw herself backward. Everyone gasped as she flew through the air, showing rather a lot of her black-stockinged legs. She landed skillfully on her feet, even though one of them was in the wastebasket.

Everyone clapped and whistled. Tod wished he could be swallowed up by the floor. Leonie responded to the applause by leaping out of the basket, leaning forward with her hands on her hips, and saying, "You shoulda seen this kid when he was three. . . ."

Two girls at the back were giggling uncontrollably. Ms. Linkman stepped in front of Leonie looking determined and in control. "Thanks, Ms. Crofton," she said. "I think it's best if you leave Tod with me. He's going to be just fine."

"Farewell, farewell, my only son," Leonie said switching character rapidly. Her face changed and softened and her accent became Irish. They could all hear her going on about her darlin' boy as Ms. Linkman escorted her out of the classroom and down the passage.

Tod was left on his own facing the class. There was a chart of Australian animals on the wall next to him. He pretended to be studying it carefully, frowning as though it was the most interesting thing he'd ever read. No one spoke to him. They were looking at each other and stifling giggles behind their hands. He couldn't think of a worse way to begin life at a new school.

He'd got through the numbat and platypus and was on to the bilby before Ms. Linkman came back into the classroom. Her face was a little pinker and she looked rather agitated. Obviously she didn't meet mothers like Leonie every day. Still, she gave Tod a nice smile. Perhaps she wouldn't hold him responsible.

"Now, Tod," she said, looking around the already over-crowded classroom, "I'm not sure just where I'm going to put you. We're rather a large class. You're going to be my thirty-second student." She raised her voice a little to address the whole class. "Can someone tell Tod what that means for us all?"

One of the girls who had been giggling at the back immediately put up her hand.

"Yes, Belinda." Tod could tell from Ms. Linkman's voice that she really liked this girl.

"We have to be patient, cooperative, and polite," Belinda said.

"Absolutely," Ms. Linkman agreed with enthusiasm. "Anyone else want to add anything? One of the boys?"

She picked a small, pale boy with big blue eyes and longish blond hair. "Adrian?"

"We don't get taught properly," he said innocently, and then looked around waiting for everyone to laugh.

Ms. Linkman pressed her lips tightly together and ignored him. "Martin?" she said to the boy next to him.

Martin was tall and wore glasses. He looked clever, Tod thought. "We have to work on our own a lot," he said, "and help each other."

"That's right," Ms. Linkman said. "Martin, can you take Tod to the activity room and bring back a chair for him. He'll have to share that table with you and Adrian for the time being. You can show him around the school on your way. I'll get everyone started on some work now," she told Tod. "And then I'll have a look at your books with you."

Martin seemed nice enough, but he was shy. He hardly said anything to Tod as they walked around the school apart from mumbling, "Resource center, canteen, oval," at the right moment. Tod couldn't think of anything to say either. So when they had picked up the chair from the activity room, where a class of very small kids was hopping around pretending to be kangaroos, they walked back to the classroom in silence.

Adrian was quite different. When Tod and Martin came into the room he was chattering away to the boy sitting behind him. As soon as Tod sat down, Adrian started talking to him.

"Was that your mother? She is so cool! Wow! I do that sort of stuff, you know, acting and all that. I go to talent school—the Silver Studio. Have you heard of it? It's really well known. I've been on TV too—Target, Venture, K-Mart—I've done ads for all of them. These are my Looks." He set his features carefully. "Pleased. Surprised. Scared."

Tod couldn't help laughing. He thought Adrian was strange but funny. And Adrian being pleased, surprised, and scared was a lot more interesting than Martin saying, "resource center, canteen, oval." He wondered if the two boys sat together because they were friends or because they were the odd ones out in the class who no one else wanted to sit next to.

He was just thinking it was most likely because they were both oddballs in their own way when Ms. Linkman loomed above him. "Now, Tod," she said briskly, "bring your chair up to the front next to my desk and we'll have a look at your work."

Tod smiled ruefully to himself when he saw Leonie had put his art folder on the top. He liked drawing and it came easily to him. Reading and writing, on the other hand, were hard, and they bored him. They seemed such a slow way to deal with the world and they made everything fixed in a way that he'd never been able to explain to anyone, but that he didn't like. Through the window behind Ms. Linkman's desk he could see right across to the hills' face and the quarries. Above the gum trees the sky was a cold winter blue. Huge white clouds with steel gray undersides were moving slowly across it. The outside world beckoned him—and it was still only the beginning of the morning. The hours till 3:30 stretched away unbearably.

He sighed and tried to listen to Ms. Linkman.

"These are excellent, Tod," she was saying looking through the drawings. He wasn't sure they were—every drawing always fell short of what he saw inside his head—but his family usually raved about them. He suspected, though, that they raved because there wasn't much else they could rave about when it came to schoolwork.

"You must like art," Ms. Linkman commented, closing up the folder and taking up one of the exercise books underneath it. "Do you like reading, too?"

"Not really," Tod confessed. He knew Leonie wouldn't have told Ms. Linkman he was no good at it. She believed in not labeling people before others had had a chance to make up their own minds about them. But it wasn't the sort of thing you could hide and Ms. Linkman would find out soon enough.

Ms. Linkman was frowning as she went on to his written expression book. Most of his stories were only two or three lines long, and he knew they had heaps of spelling mistakes in them. His math books were just as bad. They looked so messy and babyish he was ashamed of them. He stared out of the window again, trying to think himself up into the quarries, hidden in the tangled olive trees among the rocks.

"You might have a bit of catching up to do," Ms. Linkman said. She sounded rather depressed about it. Probably thinking of the thirty-one other kids and all the extra work she had to do already. Tod felt sorry for causing her more trouble. With an effort he dragged himself back from the quarries and gave her what he hoped was a reassuring smile.

She smiled back at him and picked up a math textbook. "This is where we're up to," she said. "Some of the students have worked on ahead, but most of the class are at this level. Have you done this work yet?"

She showed him the page. It looked like a foreign language. Tod shook his head. Ms. Linkman turned back a few pages. "What about this?"

It didn't look any clearer but Tod didn't want to depress her any more. "I think we did something like that," he said slowly.

"Oh good, that's not too desperate then. It won't take you long to make up the work from there."

Ms. Linkman split the class up into two groups—actually it was three groups, the fast learners, everyone else, and Tod. He was supposed to work on his own while Ms. Linkman took first the fast learner group, which Martin was in, and then everyone else, which included Adrian. He stared at the page for a while but none of it made any sense. It was much easier and more fun to whisper to Adrian.

Adrian started it. He worked very hard for about two minutes on the math questions, brow furrowed and eyes distant. Then he looked at his watch, made an exaggerated face of despair, and kicked Tod under the table. He wrote on Tod's textbook, *Where are you from?*

Sydney, Tod wrote back, hoping he'd spelled it right.

"Cool," Adrian whispered, keeping an eye on Ms. Linkman. "Why'd you come here?"

"Came to stay at my grandma's for a while. Mum's going to try and work here."

"Your dad around?"

"Gone to England on a trip."

"Wow! You should have gone with him! Catch up with Princess Di and all the Royals."

Tod tried to imagine his dad with Princess Di. She'd be

about a foot and a half taller than him. The idea made him laugh.

Ms. Linkman turned around swiftly. Adrian was deep in thought as though he'd never been anything else. Tod tried to study the page again.

Adrian's next whispered question was "Where do you live?" When Tod told him, he opened his eyes wide and rolled them back so Tod could only see the whites.

"Woo, man," he said, slipping into an American accent as easily as Leonie did. "You wanna watch you ass up there."

"Why?"

"There's some really rough kids around there." Adrian's voice returned to Australian. "There's this gang, see. My brother Shaun's part of it. They're called the Breakers. They do graffiti and stuff up and down the railway. And they play war games in the quarries. Some of them have got real guns."

Real guns, Tod thought, and he remembered the dead fox and the gunshot wound in its head.

"Stay away from the quarries," Adrian warned. "That's their territory."

Tod looked away out of the window again. He'd been planning to get up to the quarries and explore. He and Charm used to go and play there when they were younger, but they'd been too small to climb the huge rocks and the sheer face of the cliff. The idea of exploring there now that he was older was almost the only thing that made living at Grandma's endurable. He didn't want to be told it was off limits to him. And why should it be anyway? It didn't belong to anybody, not even to a tough gang who called themselves the Breakers. The name resounded in his head, all its different meanings getting mixed up together. Above the quarries the clouds looked like breakers on a huge blue sea.

His face took on an expression that his sisters would have recognized and groaned at. It was his stubborn, dogged look that meant that nothing anyone could say was going to make him change his mind or stop him from doing what he wanted to do.

The three boys stayed together most of the day. Tod decided it was as he had thought—Adrian and Martin stuck together because no one else wanted them around. They were the loners of the class. They weren't bullied or hassled particularly—he realized with relief that it wasn't that sort of school—but they weren't part of any of the groups. He himself was used to being on the outside. He'd never fitted into any of the cliques at his Sydney school.

He felt he could do worse than hang around with Adrian and Martin. He thought Martin was clever and probably kind. Adrian made him laugh, and he was generous. In his dash from the house Tod had forgotten to bring lunch with him, and then found he had no money either.

"Here," Adrian said, pulling out a couple of two-dollar coins. "I'll lend you some; you can pay me back tomorrow."

"He's always loaded," Martin commented.

"Shaun gives me lots," Adrian said. Then he squinted sideways at Tod and whispered out the side of his mouth, "To keep my mouth shut!" When they had bought themselves a pie and a drink, he said confidingly to Tod, "Martin's afraid of them."

"Who?" Tod replied.

"The Breakers."

"No, I'm not," Martin said. "I think they're morons, that's all." But he said it in an angry painful way that made Tod think perhaps he was afraid of them. He remembered the year at his last school when he had been really afraid of a group of older boys, had walked miles out of his way rather than pass them in the street, and had dreaded going to school because of the stupid little torments they put on him, throwing his bag on the roof or into the road, tripping him up, getting his lunch out and stamping on it. He couldn't now believe he'd put up with it, and never told anyone about it, not even Dad, but back then it had seemed something you couldn't change or escape from, like the weather.

He felt a sense of kinship with Martin, and he realized he was starting to hate the Breakers. It must have been them who shot the fox. They claimed the quarries as their own territory. Daydreaming through the long afternoon, tired after the broken night, he began to spin a story to himself in which he took on the gang and defeated them, avenging the death of the fox.

He tried to listen to Ms. Linkman explaining the weather experiments the class had been doing, but inside his head he was roaming the quarries with the foxes.

THREE

Over the next few weeks the Croftons settled into their new life in Grandma's house. Tod got used to the nighttime noises, and the trains hardly ever woke him up anymore. Grandma grumbled from time to time, especially at Charm, but she also admitted that she enjoyed the company and that it made life interesting having young people around. Dallas worked as hard as she ever did, and seemed happy with her new teachers. Tod helped Grandma around the place. He liked being outside and he found she knew a lot about chopping wood, putting in posts and stuff like that, as well as looking after animals and plants.

He fed the poultry and cut the grass, and hung out at school with Martin and Adrian. At home he spent a lot of time trying to make friends with Inkspot, and gradually the old cat became more trusting.

No one knew much about what Charm was doing. She kept herself to herself. When they were younger, both at primary school, she and Tod had been good mates and had done a lot of things together, but since she went to high school she didn't seem to be interested in him anymore.

Partly because Grandma was around and partly because Leonie was working, the children saw less of their mother. Leonie found a part-time day job giving sales pitches in a department store. Tod and Dallas went in to hear her one

Saturday morning. Dallas said she was really good, but Tod found it sad watching her talking and making jokes with no one really listening. At night Leonie tried out her comedy routines in pubs and clubs. Occasionally she would have a good night and come home elated, but more often she was depressed and full of doubt in the mornings.

"Wasting your time," Grandma told her. "No one wants to hear jokes about childbirth and mothers and sex—well, not sex from the woman's point of view. None of that's funny, anyway," she added. "It's bloody tragic, if you ask me."

"That's just why it's funny," Leonie replied. "If people didn't laugh they'd cut their own throats. Grim but hilarious, that's what life is."

Tod liked that. It sounded like what he knew already about the good times and the bad times. If life was grim but hilarious he thought he could cope with it. It was real—not like the stuff in books and on TV which told you that problems could always be solved and things always ended happily. Sometimes things ended happily and sometimes they didn't, but either way Leonie was right. The best way to deal with them was to laugh at them.

Sometimes it was easier said than done. He wondered if it got easier with practice.

Twice a letter came from his father. Dallas read them out to Tod. The letters were long and entertaining, full of stories about the family in England, old haunts and the sights Laurie had seen, but neither of them said when he was coming back.

The postman came in the afternoon, on a motorbike. From the classroom Tod could hear the motorbike whine as it went from house to house, and he always hoped it would bring another letter from his father, but most days he was disappointed. Then life just seemed a little bit grimmer, not hilarious at all.

He got into the habit of going to school the long way around and visiting the grave of the dead fox. That part of the little reserve became a special place for him. The winter rains had filled the creek and it chattered over the stones at the bottom of the gully. Often he heard frogs croaking. As the days grew longer flowers started to appear, vivid orange and yellow nasturtiums and two different sorts of white flowers; one smelled like onions and the other looked like the sweet-smelling freesias that were coming up in Grandma's front garden. The place had a lot of other strong smells, apart from the onion flower, like the muddy smell of the creek and the faint whiff of decay from the dead fox.

Tod ignored Adrian's warning and spent a lot of time exploring the quarries. He was beginning to map out the whole area inside his head. It was much bigger than he'd thought. From the school he could see the main quarry that dominated the side of the hill, but once you were up there you found there were lots of other little quarries, and further around the hillside the wild area went on for miles, almost like real bush, right up to where the train line went into the tunnel, and beyond.

There was a lane that led past the depot to the houses further up the hill—a shortcut to the station for the people who lived up there. Beyond the cyclone fence at the back of the depot a path twisted away down the gully, through a tangle of olive bushes and long grass where nasturtiums ran wild. It was the same gully, really, that continued on through to the little reserve where Tod had buried the fox, but the depot had been built across it. Grandma said she thought it must have been filled in years ago with the rubble from the quarries. Above the depot, in the wild part, a bank had been built across the creek, to stop flooding, Grandma said. In winter the creek flowed under a steel grill through the drain that had been laid for it under the bank, emerged for a couple of hundred yards to go racing over rocks and boulders, and then disappeared again into another drain that led right under the depot and the railway line to come out in Tod's reserve.

In the floor of the little valley beyond the bank there was a clump of trees that Tod found out were ashes. He liked the way they grew—they looked like a family. There was one big tree right by the creek that must have been the original one, and all around it were younger saplings like children. Even when he had first started exploring while it was still winter, the ash trees had black buds on them which were starting to burst into spiky green leaves.

Olives had also invaded the whole area. Further up the creek they formed a tangled mass that was almost impossible to get through unless you went on hands and knees and followed the tracks that animals had made. Tod went through there sometimes, as quietly as a fox, wondering if he was following a fox's track.

Despite Adrian's warning he never saw anyone else there, though sometimes he heard a bird shriek or a stick break, and had the feeling he was being watched. He didn't see any animals either, apart from magpies, finches, and blackbirds, until one day on his way to school he saw something near the fox's grave.

He knew at once it was another fox, even though it was standing quite still and fearless as if it belonged there, not slinking around furtively, in the way he would have expected a fox to. Its mouth was slightly open and he could see its pointy pink tongue. Its brush swung gently from side to side. It was bigger than the dead fox and its color was much brighter, a brilliant russet brown. It heard Tod, turned its head, and looked him straight in the eyes.

Tod stood frozen and looked back at the fox. He felt as if something wild leaped from the animal's eyes and planted itself deep inside him. It was the most exciting moment of his life. He could feel his heart beating. Then the fox's sharp face softened—almost as though it recognized me, Tod said to himself afterward. He felt he could just step forward and the fox would allow him to touch it. But before he could move the fox turned and trotted calmly away. It stopped once on the top of the bank and looked back at Tod, and then it padded across the railway line.

Tod ran up the bank after it. He could see it still trotting at the same even pace along the track, and then it disappeared around the curve.

He wanted to find out more about the foxes. He wanted to know them better. He combed the quarries looking for traces of them, but he never saw any up there, though he was sure that was where they lived. He was frustrated because he wasn't really clear about what he was looking for: he realized he didn't know enough about foxes to know if he was looking in the right places. He needed to be able to recognize fox clues so that he could track and find them.

Nobody at home knew much about them. Grandma was alarmed when he told her he'd seen the fox in the reserve and they spent a couple of hours reinforcing the old chook run.

"I've lost a whole lot of chooks to those devils in the past," Grandma told him. "I don't want to lose these ones. You never want to see that, Tod, the mess left after a fox has been among the poultry. They go mad. They don't just kill one bird and take it away to eat. They kill the lot. It's terrible."

She phoned the council, though Tod begged her not to, and spent a long time trying to find the right department.

"They've got a long-term plan," she said when she finally got off the phone. "Long-term, my foot. What they need to do is come out here with a couple of shotguns and get the blighters. I should have kept my old gun," she grumbled. "Then I could have sat up at night and potted them."

"Don't worry," Leonie said, seeing Tod's face. "The council will never get around to doing anything, and Grandma doesn't really mean it."

"Oh, don't I?" Grandma retorted. "Just let one of them come near my poultry and you'll see if I meant it or not."

"Foxes are a terrible pest," Dallas said, looking up from the table where she was studying. "That's why there's no native wildlife left around here. The foxes and the feral cats have killed everything."

"It's not their fault," Tod said, feeling he had to stand up for the foxes. "They've got to eat something."

"They don't belong here," Dallas replied. "They should never have been brought here."

"Where did they come from?" he demanded. "Who brought them here?"

"I don't know," she said, distracted, frowning at her physics textbook. "Go and ask in your library. They should have some books on foxes."

"Come to the resource center," Tod said to Martin at recess the next day.

Martin looked surprised. He quite often spent recess and lunch in the resource center, but Tod and Adrian never did.

"I want to get some books," Tod went on. "You can help me find them."

"What do you want books for?" Adrian said. "You never read anything."

"I want to find out about something," Tod said. "It's not against the law, is it?"

"All depends," Adrian replied in a rather sinister voice. "All depends on what you want to find out and why." When Tod didn't answer he went on, "They've heard you've been sneaking around their territory, you know. They don't like it. They've told me to tell you to stay away."

"Who?" Tod asked, though he knew very well.

Adrian lowered his voice. "The Breakers," he hissed. "Shaun told me to tell you. They've seen you up there and they're warning you."

"They don't own the place," Tod retorted. "Anyone can go there. Anyway, I don't believe they've seen me. I've never seen anyone up there."

"No one sees them," Adrian said. "They're almost invisible. But they've got eyes everywhere. You can't escape them."

"Jeez, Adrian, you're full of it," Tod groaned.

Adrian shrugged and rolled his eyes upward. "Just warning you, mate."

Martin had been pursuing his own line of thought. "He wouldn't go to the library to find out about your brother's stupid gang," he put in, "because no one's written any books about them and what's more they never will." He smiled triumphantly at Adrian.

"You're right," Adrian said. "But they'll write books about us, won't they, Marty, my main man? Because we're going to be famous!" He stopped and looked seriously at Tod. "But what about Tod? Do you reckon Tod'll make it into the history books too?"

"Not a chance," Martin said, grinning at Tod. "He doesn't

even know how to find a book in the library."

"So come and help me," Tod said impatiently.

"What sort of books do you want?" Martin said as they went into the resource center.

"I want to find out about foxes," Tod replied.

"Animals are in the five nineties," Martin said. He knew the entire Dewey decimal system by heart. He and Tod went off to look on the shelves.

Adrian's system was to go and ask the librarian. Ms. Livetti was in the process of transferring books on to the computer, and she was not in a helpful mood. She told Adrian to go look it up himself.

There didn't seem to be anything about foxes on the shelves. Martin took down one of the big reference books and read out what it said to Tod. It wasn't very helpful, just telling them that the fox was a small reddish brown mammal native to every continent except Australia and Antarctica.

Adrian came up looking pleased with himself, holding several books in his hands. Martin took them and read the titles: *Fox at School, Fantastic Mr. Fox, The Tale of Mr. Tod.*

"It's a book about Tod," Adrian yelped, making Ms. Livetti turn around and frown at them. "It's his story. He's made it into print already! The tale of Mr. Tod!"

Tod opened the little book. The fox was wearing clothes. "These are just stories," he said, disappointed. "These aren't about real foxes." He looked at *Fox at School.* "Foxes don't do this sort of thing," he said. The books made him angry. They had nothing to do with the dead fox with a bullet through its skull, nothing to do with the wild feeling that had jumped into him from the live fox's eyes.

Ms. Livetti came up to them. Perhaps she was sorry she'd been sharp with Adrian before, or perhaps she just wanted to get rid of them. "What are you boys looking for?"

"He wants to find some books on foxes," Martin said, indicating Tod.

"It's for a project," Adrian added impressively.

"Ugh, foxes," Ms. Livetti said. "Nasty creatures. I don't think we've got much on foxes. They aren't native Australian animals, you know. Why don't you do a project on a native animal? We've got lots about them." She stepped over to the animal section and took out a couple of books. "Numbat? Wallaby?"

"It's really foxes I'm interested in," Tod said stubbornly.

"What about sharks?" Ms. Livetti offered.

Tod shook his head.

"I like sharks," Adrian said. "This is a great book. It's got the coolest pictures. Look!" He showed Tod and Martin a photo of a man with tooth marks all over the upper half of his body. By the time they had finished admiring it Ms. Livetti had given up on them and gone back to the computer.

They trailed out of the resource center as the siren went for the end of recess. "I'll have a look at home," Martin said to Tod as they returned to the classroom. "We've got lots of books about wildlife and all that stuff."

When Tod walked around to the back door of Grandma's house that afternoon he was amazed to hear loud music blaring out. Inside he found Charm dancing to SAFM in the front room, which doubled as a sitting room and their mother's bedroom. She had draped one of Leonie's shawls over her shoulders, and she held another one over her head as she swayed from side to side.

She didn't appear to see Tod and when he shouted at her she pretended not to hear him. He walked over to the radio and turned it down.

"Where's everyone?" he said.

"Don't turn it down!" Charm shrieked. "This is such a cool song! Come on, come and dance too!"

He dropped his bag on the floor and began to bop around. Charm crossed the room to the radio in a series of hops and jumps and turned it up again. They danced more and more wildly, each trying to outdo the other in daring and inventiveness. When the music finished and the ads came on they collapsed in a heap on the floor, giggling helplessly. It reminded Tod of how things used to be with Charm. He realized he'd hardly seen her since they'd moved to Grandma's, and hardly said more to her than "get out of the bathroom" and "have you nicked my pencil case?"

"Woo!" Charm yelled. "That's better. This poor old house was starving for some good music. It needed shaking up a bit. Everything in it's dozed off."

They were laughing so much it was some time before they realized someone was knocking on the front door.

"Who's at the door?" Tod said.

"How'm I supposed to know? Go and open it and you'll find out!"

"Well, get off me, and I'll be able to."

The music was still blaring out as Tod opened the door. Outside was Martin, looking surprised.

"I thought this was your grandma's house," he said when Tod brought him in.

"It is."

"Does she let you play the radio that loud? My grandma doesn't."

"She's out," Tod replied, hoping that it was true and not that poor old Grandma was trying to have a nap on her bed. "This is my sister Charmian. We always call her Charm. This is Martin."

Charm was still lying on the floor swathed in shawls. Despite her greenish hair she looked like a model from a magazine. Tod realized with a shock that she was pretty in a unique way. She looked sensational. Martin couldn't take his eyes off her.

"Hi, Martin," Charm said.

"Hello," he stammered. Then there was silence. Charm began singing along with the radio. Finally Martin remembered why he'd come and said to Tod, "I found some stuff in a book. You know, about the foxes."

The book was about tracks and signs. Martin opened it and showed a page to Tod. "See this is all about foxes and how to know where they are and how to track them. I'll leave it with you and you can read it. I can't stay now. I've got a music lesson."

"Music lesson!" Charm repeated. "What do you play?"

"The trumpet," Martin said, going bright red. He looked as if he was going to say something else, but then he closed his mouth again and nodded to Tod. "See you tomorrow at school," he said. At the door he turned and said boldly, "See you, Charm!" Then he bolted. They heard the front door slam. Charm started giggling again.

"Cool dude!"

"He's nice," Tod said defensively.

"Never said he wasn't! What's the book?"

"Will you read this page to me?" Tod asked her, turning the radio down. He knew it would take him ages to work out what it said, and he was in a hurry. He thought if he could find something out he could go up to the quarry before it got dark and try it out.

Charm sat up and took the book from him. "Let's have a look." She skimmed over the pages. "Why're you so interested in foxes?"

"There are some living in the quarry. I wanted to try and see them."

"It's great up there," Charm said. "I like the quarry."

"I've never seen you up there," Tod said, surprised.

"That's 'cause I go when you're at school."

"Charm." He groaned. "You promised Mum you wouldn't cut school this term."

"I've only done it a couple of times," she said. "Don't tell her. She'll only get upset. Anyway the school sucks. No one's learning anything. It's a waste of time going. And there's a kind of gang of boys—they're such idiots."

"The Breakers?"

"I don't know what they call themselves. Probably something moronic like that."

"Do they hassle you?"

"They hassle everyone." But Tod, watching Charm's face, saw it tauten.

"They give you heaps, don't they?"

"It's so boring," she said. "I hate it. I wish we'd never left Sydney."

"There were gangs there," Tod pointed out.

"Yeah, but they didn't hassle me. I belonged there. I feel so different here. I don't fit in at all. I say words wrong and everyone laughs at me. I don't know any of the cool places. I haven't got any friends."

This sounded so unlike Charm that Tod was alarmed. He didn't know what to say. He tried to think of something hilarious but nothing would come.

"Don't worry," Charm said, seeing his scowling face. "I'll survive. But that's why I have to cut school now and then, so don't dob on me, okay?"

"Okay," Tod said.

"Better swear it, or I won't read your fox stuff."

"Yeah, yeah, I swear it!"

She read out about how you recognized a fox's tracks. They were different from a dog's in that the paws were smaller and neater and, if you drew a line from the tips of the outer digits, it didn't cross the middle digits, as it did in a dog. Tod frowned at the pictures trying to imprint them on his memory.

dog's paw print   fox's paw print

"This is interesting," Charm said. "You can call foxes to come to you."

Tod was enthralled with the idea. "How do you do it?"

"You find an area where you think the foxes are and make a noise like a hurt rabbit—a sort of squeal, I suppose. Then the fox comes to see what it is."

"Do you have to do anything else?"

"Rub yourself all over with leaves and dirt so the fox can't smell you. It's best to do it at dawn or sunset."

"How do you know where they are?"

"The book says you smell 'em out! So use your nose." Charm sniffed noisily. "Pooh! I think I can smell one in here!"

"Don't fool around," Tod begged her. "Is there any other way of finding them?"

"You look for their scats."

"What are scats?" Tod asked.

"Their poopoo, dummy!" Charm made a face. "This is

rather gross. Here, take your book and go look for your foxes. I need to do some more dancing."

Tod could hear the radio blaring out again as he changed. He put on his oldest clothes so it wouldn't matter if he rubbed dirt into them. His jeans were getting too short, he noticed with surprise. He must be growing.

Outside it was cold. The sky was almost covered with heavy gray clouds. Only toward the west was it clear, where a pale yellow sun lay low in the sky. He felt he should hurry. It must be nearly sunset. A few drops of rain hit his face as he crossed the railway line. The dump and depot were deserted. At the end of the afternoon while he and Charm were dancing, the workers would have taken off in their noisy convoy of cars. He looked through the high wire gates, remembered the weird voice alarm, and wondered what it took to set it off. He went past the gates carefully, just in case, and then jogged up the lane.

Someone had been around with a spray can. There were new tags on the road sign at the top of the lane and on the council sign forbidding skateboards and bicycles. Tod looked around, a little nervous. He remembered what Adrian had said about the Breakers having eyes everywhere. Again he had the feeling someone was watching him. For a moment he thought about turning around and going home. He could just imagine how cozy it would seem at Grandma's right now with the TV going and someone, probably Dallas, cooking tea. But more than anything he wanted to see the foxes, so he slipped around the end of the fence and down into the gully.

By the time he had gone past the bank and through the tangled olive bushes, it was much darker. The pale sun had given up the struggle and disappeared behind the clouds.

Underfoot there were still patches of mud from the rain the day before, and Tod studied these carefully for paw prints. At last he found what he was looking for, the neat paw with the space between the digits where you could easily draw a line. He squatted down and studied it. It looked just like in the book. He felt great looking at it. He really was going to see a fox. There had been one along this path just recently. It might be just up ahead of him.

Then he found the scat. It was small and shiny black, as though the fox had been eating olives. Just beyond the scat the creek formed a little pool, and above the pool a very faint track led up the hill. In the soft damp ground at the side of the pool were two more paw prints. Tod imagined the fox stopping to drink, and then heading away upward, back to its den.

He put his finger in the water and tasted it. I'm drinking the country, he thought, just like the fox does, and he had a sudden flash of how it felt to be wild and to live directly off the earth, without food in shops or water coming out of taps, without the whole superstructure that made up the world he lived in and that had nothing whatsoever to do with the life that the wild creatures lived.

He scooped up mud from the creek and rubbed it into his clothes. Then he rubbed it all over his face and hair in a kind of frenzy.

He went on all fours up the steep slope, following the fox track. After a long climb the ground leveled out and the olives became less dense. Ahead of him Tod could see a small clearing. He sniffed the air. He could smell the mud from the creek that he was plastered with, and behind that the honey smell of the flowering wattle and the balsamy smell of gum trees, but he wasn't sure if he could smell anything like a fox's den.

The book had said he should try to hide downwind from

the den, but he didn't know where the den was, though if it was going to be anywhere he thought it might be back toward the hills, in among the boulders. He put his face up trying to feel the wind. It was blowing from the south as it usually did at this time of year, icy cold as if it had come straight from Antarctica. If the fox's den was where he thought it was, it was going to be practically impossible to approach it downwind, unless he dropped in on it from the sky.

He realized how clever the fox was.

Then he realized something else that he hadn't thought about before—he was going to feel like an idiot sitting making noises like a rabbit. Again he seriously considered going home. He looked around wondering what to do, wishing he'd waited till Martin or Adrian could have come with him. But it was the sort of thing you could only do on your own. If there were other people there they'd only chatter and frighten the fox away, especially Adrian . . . he was smiling to himself thinking how much Adrian would be chattering if he were there now, when he saw a perfect hiding spot, in among the olives. It was as close to being downwind as it was possible to get. He could hide in there and call the fox.

He went in on all fours and crouched down. It was a little warmer out of the wind. He could hear it soughing outside in the treetops. Magpies were warbling, and from further down the hill a blackbird shrieked a warning note.

Tod gave a series of screams like a hurt animal, shrill and high-pitched. When he stopped the silence was amazing. The birds had gone quiet. Even the wind seemed to have dropped. It was as if the whole area was listening.

He screamed again into the silence. Then he listened. The blackbird made him jump by shrieking again. He felt as if he was calling something alarming toward himself. But he wanted to see the fox. And now he'd started there was no point stopping. For a third time he made the high, unearthly shriek, wondering if it sounded anything like a rabbit in distress.

Down the hill track he heard a slight sound, a stick breaking perhaps as someone trod on it. Tod froze. He was staring in the direction of the noise when something made him turn around and look back through the olives. Through their tangled grayish branches he could just make out the shape of the big fox. It was standing about twenty yards away from him, staring straight at him. Their eyes met and the wild feeling jumped between them as it had done before. Tod sat stockstill, enraptured. He had called the fox and it had come to him.

For about twenty seconds neither of them moved. Then Tod heard something coming up the hill. He heard whispered voices, and someone hiss urgently, "Shut up!"

Looking back from his hiding place he saw three boys emerge into the little clearing. Two of them were dressed in army camouflage pants and green sweatshirts. The other was in black jeans and wore a red-and-green bandana around his head. They moved with quick, precise movements, and constantly turned their heads to survey the land around them. They couldn't have been much older than fourteen or fifteen, he thought, but they looked like soldiers. The oldest-looking army camouflage one, who Tod immediately guessed was Adrian's brother, Shaun, was carrying a roughly sawn-off shotgun.

He looked a little like Adrian, or like Adrian would be when he was older, with the same blond hair and bright blue eyes. The blue eyes looked sharp and bold, and Tod didn't like them. He felt, rather than heard, the fox depart and, without thinking, he turned and wriggled as quietly as he could after it.

He heard one of the boys say quietly, "There's one," and the gun cracked. Something whistled through the bushes to the left of him, and he just had time to think with surprise that he was being shot at, before instinct took over and he moved faster and more quietly than he ever had in his life.

At first he had to go on all fours, but then the trail emerged from the olives and began to wind up the hill back toward the big quarry. Here he could stand and run properly. But he seemed to run much further than he thought he should and he didn't recognize the area he was running through at all. It looked darker and wilder, and the gum trees were being replaced by ashes, like the ones in the creek bed but much bigger, and so dark they were blotting out the light altogether, until he was running through almost complete darkness.

I'm dreaming, he thought with a sort of mad relief. This is a dream and I'll wake up in a minute. But the darkness cleared, and he was still running, and in front of him he could see the huge fox—it really was huge, bigger than a German shepherd. He caught one last glimpse of its white-tipped brush as it vanished behind a massive boulder. When Tod rounded the boulder he found he was standing before a huge pile of rocks like a fortress wall. There was no sign of the fox, but when he dropped to his knees he saw a way through the rocks like a tunnel. He could just squeeze through it. On the other side he came out on the floor of a quarry he had not known existed.

The upper part of the cliff face was lit by the last rays of the sun, which had come out from the clouds just in time to set. Where Tod stood the quarry was dark and chilly. He shivered. He thought he should go back before it got dark, before Dallas and Mum and Grandma started to worry about him.

There was no sign of the fox, but at least he had seen it and followed it. He thought he would take a quick look around and see if he could find its den. Then he would run home—and hope the Breakers had gone by then.

Up ahead he saw a flicker of movement. He thought it might be the fox, but then flames suddenly sprang into life. Someone was there—someone who had just lit a campfire. The flames made the surrounding quarry look much darker. They burned warm and welcoming in the gathering twilight.

Tod took a step toward the fire, but then he thought better of it. Who could it be up there? He didn't want to meet strangers in the dark quarry at nightfall, and he definitely didn't want to meet the Breakers, though if it were the gang he couldn't imagine how they had got into the quarry ahead of him. He didn't feel like investigating any further. It was definitely time to go home.

He wriggled back through the tunnel, and past the huge boulder. He noticed he could smell the fox strongly, as though this sense had improved. As he went back down the hill and through the olives he thought he could sniff the acrid smell of guns, and a sweat and cigarette smell from the humans. People, he corrected himself. Why had he thought humans?

The people smell was fading. He knew the gang had left the quarries. He followed the way back swiftly, not getting lost once, even though it was nearly dark by the time he got to the creek. It was the darkness of real ordinary night falling, not the mysterious unreal darkness of the quarry that shouldn't have been where it was. He shook his head, puzzled, as he trotted down the lane and crossed the railway line. But at the front gate the best smell of all drove all other thoughts except hunger out of his mind. Dallas had made macaroni and cheese for tea.

FOUR

Tod had forgotten the mud he'd smeared all over himself. He was greeted with howls of protest from his family.

"Toddy, what have you been doing?" Leonie wailed. "You're filthy."

"And it stinks," Dallas said. "You'd better get in the shower quick. Here, take your dirty clothes off and I'll put them in the tub to soak."

"But the shower'll be freezing," Tod protested. "And I'm starving."

"What happened to you?" Leonie said. "Did you fall in the creek?"

"He was calling foxes," Charm put in. "You have to rub mud over yourself so they don't smell you." She made it sound like a perfectly reasonable thing to do. "Did it work?" she said to Tod. "Did any come?"

His voice was muffled as he pulled his sweatshirt over his head. "Yeah, I saw a big one. And I think I found where its den is." He wondered whether to mention the gang and the gunshot, and then decided against it. Mum would worry and forbid him to go to the quarries anymore and Grandma would probably call the cops.

"Calling foxes!" Grandma said. "Never heard anything like it. You want to tell 'em to go away, not to call 'em to come to you. You'd better not call any around here." But she didn't really sound angry, and when Tod got his head out of his clothes he could see she had a smile on her face. She puzzled him. He was never sure if she approved of him or not, but right now she was looking as if she did.

Dallas was clicking her tongue as she took the muddy clothes into the laundry.

"Don't worry about it," Grandma said. "Boys will be boys. Just good clean mud. Nothing wrong with that."

"I think he should wash his own clothes," Leonie called out to Dallas. "And really, Ma, don't you know that's the most sexist thing to say."

"What, good clean mud?" Grandma replied in surprise. "Nothing sexist about that."

"No, you know what I mean! 'Boys will be boys.' That's what everyone says to excuse boys being rough and violent and all that stuff. It's nonsense. They don't have to be like that. It's just the way society trains them to be. And I think everyone, male or female, should learn to do their own washing. His sister's not going to look after him forever."

"I wouldn't mind," Dallas said, coming back into the kitchen.

Charm groaned. "Dallas, you spoil him. He's never going to do anything for himself. He'll never be a SNAG at this rate."

"What on earth is a SNAG?" Grandma demanded.

"A Sensitive New Age Guy. That's what all the girls want these days. Apart from black basketball players," she added. "But I expect some people can be both."

"A snag is a sausage, as far as I'm concerned," Grandma said. "Always has been, always will be."

"It can't always have been," Charm said, winking at Tod. "There must have been some stage in prehistory when a snag wasn't a sausage. In fact, it wouldn't have been anything at all."

"This is great stuff," Leonie said. "You guys are fantastic. I just have to listen to you and write it all down, and bang I've got a whole routine."

"Wish you'd pay us for it," Charm complained.

"Soon as I get paid I will, my darling daughter," Leonie said ruefully. "Toddy, you're shivering. Go and have a shower and get some dry clothes on."

"And hurry up so's we can eat," Charm yelled after him. "Mum, can't I start?"

"No, wait for Tod," he heard her say as he headed for the shower. "I want us all to eat together. We hardly ever have a chance to do things together as a family."

"We have breakfast together," Charm was arguing as he shut the bathroom door. He didn't hear his mother's answer.

The shower was not as cold as it might have been. As he washed the mud out of his hair he thought about everything that had happened. There had been the fox, and the gang, but there was something else that was bothering him. Who was the person who had lit the fire in the quarry he hadn't known was there? And why hadn't he ever been in it before? And why, when he thought of the darkness and the ash trees did he feel . . . not exactly frightened but in awe of something. It was all mysterious and not at all ordinary, as if he had stumbled on something that had never occurred to him before, something he'd never even dreamed of.

Then the shower did run cold so he stopped thinking in a hurry and got out and dried himself.

"So how was school?" Leonie asked him when he was

clean and dressed and sitting at the table. Dallas was serving out big steaming bowls of macaroni and cheese with sliced tomatoes and grated cheese on top. It smelled wonderful. Tod's mouth was watering.

"It was fine," he said.

"Anything interesting happen?"

"Nothing funny," he said. "I went to the resource center."

"That's pretty funny," Charm muttered.

Tod remembered something. "Did you name me after a book, Mum?"

"No, we named you after the river in Alice Springs."

"Is that where he was conceived?" Charm questioned.

"Well, it was, as a matter of fact," Leonie said. "But your dad spelled it wrong on the registration form, so you only got one *d* instead of two."

"There's a book in the library called *The Tale of Mr. Tod.*"

"Oh, I remember that," Dallas said. "It's by Beatrix Potter. Do you remember when I had a craze for collecting all those things? I had all the books and all the little animals. They were gorgeous." She took a big mouthful of macaroni and cheese and looked at her mother. "Where is all that stuff, Mum? We didn't get rid of it, did we?"

"It's all stored in Sydney. We'll get it back when we decide what to do and where to live. Don't worry, Dallas, I wouldn't chuck any of your precious things out!"

"*The Tale of Mr. Tod,*" said Charm, "that's the one about the fox, isn't it?"

"*Tod* is an old word for fox," Leonie said. "I think it's Scottish."

"Well, the world of crazy coincidences," Charm said. "So your name means fox, Tod. And you never knew."

He grinned at her. It made him feel very happy.

"You'll change into one if you're not careful," she warned him. "Specially if you go around covering yourself in mud and calling them."

There were a few moments of silence while they all ate away steadily. "This is good, Dallas," Grandma said. "You're a good cook, girl."

"You don't have to sound so surprised," Leonie said, joking.

"She's your daughter, isn't she?" Grandma teased back. "You never cooked a meal like this when you were seventeen. Too busy chasing the lads."

"Was she?" Charm said with interest. "Tell us about it, Grandma. Did she cut school and smoke and do all those wicked things people used to do?"

"She was a bit of a tearaway," Grandma said.

"No giving away all my secrets," Leonie begged.

"You tell the whole world and his dog your secrets every night in the pub! Got no secrets left, as far as I can see!"

"Oh, that was a good one, Ma! I've got to hand it to you, you're quick. No wonder I'm a comedian with a mother like that. I had all those years of training in this very kitchen. Now I'm going to change the subject! I've asked Tod how school was, and we had a very interesting conversation about Beatrix Potter and foxes. Now I'll ask you, Charm. How was school?"

"You're weird," Charm said, smiling, "and school was okay."

"Did you go?" Leonie said.

"Mum, yes, I went."

"No hassles?"

Charm shook her head.

"No hot gossip from the adolescent world?"

"If there was I wouldn't tell you. No one wants their affairs turned into one of your comic routines!"

Leonie frowned. "Does that mean you wouldn't tell me if there was anything wrong?"

Charm didn't say anything. No one else spoke. Tod realized the jokey conversation had suddenly turned serious.

"Anyone want some more?" Dallas said brightly, brandishing the serving ladle.

"Dallas, don't try and change the subject. I want an answer. Would *you* tell me if there was anything wrong?"

"If it was serious enough," Dallas said slowly.

"What does serious enough mean?" Leonie demanded, her eyes going dark and huge.

"Serious enough that I thought you wouldn't use it." Dallas tried to smile. "Sorry, Mum, but I think we all feel the same."

"You don't want me to work!" Leonie said tragically. "You don't want me to succeed."

"They just don't want you using their lives to make jokes from," Grandma said. "And you can't blame them."

"But our lives are all so funny," Leonie pleaded. "And I make jokes about my own life too. I make more jokes about myself than about anyone else.

"At least I'm doing something," she went on, getting more serious when she saw that no one else was smiling. "I'm trying to do something with my life, something different and interesting. I'm trying to express myself and find some meaning in things."

"You haven't changed since you were seventeen," Grandma said, shaking her head, but she said it affectionately. "You always did want to make people sit up and take notice of you. Your aunt, Carol," she told the children, "she was more like

Dallas here, quieter and more homey. But your mum was a tearaway, like I said. She was afraid of nothing."

"I took after you," Leonie said.

"Well, maybe you did! There've always been strong women in our family. Look at my mother—lost her husband in the First War, and ran the farm by herself for twenty years. She was going to hand it over to my brother, but the Second War started and he went and got himself killed in it, so she kept the farm on herself for another twenty years, with only May to help her. She was a tough old thing, and so stubborn."

"Is that the May that the chook's named after?" Tod asked.

"Yes, that's the one." Grandma cackled. "Good thing she never comes to visit me; she might not care for that. But once Mother died and May got away she was never going to come back again. She's stuck up there in Queensland with her rich widower to keep her company. She'll never come back. And good luck to her."

Tod thought about this. So people did leave their families and never come back. He wanted to say something about Dad, but there seemed to be something stopping him from speaking. Luckily Charm spoke for him.

"So when do we make the big decision about what we're going to do and where we're going to live?" she said abruptly.

"I don't know yet," Leonie said. "I just need a bit of time to wait and see what happens."

"Well, is Dad coming back or is he going to stay in England?"

Leonie looked troubled. "I don't know that either. We just have to wait and see."

"I don't like it," Charm said loudly. "I don't like this waiting. I want to get on with my life. I can't do that when everyone's just sitting around waiting. I hate it."

"Look, I know it's hard for you," Leonie said even louder. "But it's hard for me too and I'm doing the best I can."

"Don't fight, don't fight," Dallas begged. "It'll spoil the dinner."

"No one's fighting," Charm yelled. "I'm just trying to tell you how I feel. But you're not interested. None of you are. None of you give a stuff about how I might be feeling." She leaped up, pushing her chair back violently, and ran out of the room.

"She must be getting her period," Leonie said. "She's so moody at the moment."

"Mum," Dallas groaned, "there are other reasons for being upset, you know."

"I'm doing the best I can," Leonie said again, looking at Dallas, her eyes moist with tears.

"We know you are. Don't worry about it. We'll be fine here. And Dad will come back, I know he will. And if he doesn't we'll all go to England to live."

"You wouldn't really, would you?" Grandma said in alarm.

"I don't know," Leonie said, and sniffed. "I just have to wait and see."

"Go and sit down and put your feet up," Dallas told her. "I'll make you a cup of tea and Tod and I'll do the washing up."

"Cup of tea, phooey," Grandma said. "We need something stronger than that. Come on, Leo, I'll get you a drink."

While Dallas and Tod were cleaning up in the kitchen, they could hear Grandma and Leonie talking away cheerfully in the living room. Leonie went out to her gig looking quite animated, and then Grandma played cards with Tod while Dallas tried to do some studying. But Charm didn't reappear and Tod had the uncomfortable feeling that nothing had been settled, because nothing had ever really been discussed. That was how it always was with Charm and Leonie. They flared up so quickly they never really got to say anything to each other before the conversation turned into a fight. Now he suspected Charm would be even more likely to cut school, or get into some other trouble.

He went to bed with mixed feelings. Part of him was wildly excited about seeing the fox, and planning to go back and track it some more. Part of him was worried about his family, wondering what was going to happen to them and when Dad would come back. He didn't dare think about the horrible if . . . if Laurie didn't come back. Dallas had said they'd all go to England, but then they would be strangers there too, and it would probably be far worse than being strangers in Adelaide.

Part of him kept going back to the fact that someone had shot at him that day. His mind refused to take it in properly. It made him feel like laughing and shaking at the same time. He thought about the boys in the gang—he could see the three of them clearly. Shaun with his blond hair and blue eyes, and the other two—one of them very dark with tanned skin and black eyes, a lean face with a big nose rather like a greyhound's, and the other stocky, a nondescript sort of person with a thickish white neck and short cropped, mousy colored hair.

He wasn't sure if he hated the Breakers or not. They scared him but they also made him feel excited and alive. However, his last thought before he finally went to sleep was not of the gang. It was of the fox and that wild feeling. Tod stretched his legs in his sleep as if he were running, and his teeth showed as he snarled.

FIVE

At school the next morning Adrian wouldn't talk to Tod and Martin. He turned his back on them and made a big show of talking to the boys behind him. He was even more hyperactive than usual and Ms. Linkman finally had to send him to the time-out area to calm down. He avoided Tod all day, but at lunch every time Tod looked across the school yard Adrian was watching him intently.

"What's up with him?" he asked Martin. "Have I done something?"

Martin shrugged. "He's always like this. One week he's your best friend, the next he doesn't want to know you. It's just the way he is. He's probably got it into his head that you've done something against him—half the time it's just something he's made up. You know how he's always acting and showing off. He lives in a world of his own."

"I thought it might have something to do with his brother," Tod said.

Martin didn't say anything for a few minutes. He chewed deliberately on his sandwich. When he'd finished he carefully wrapped up the paper and lobbed it toward the garbage can.

"Why should it?" he said finally.

"Don't tell anyone," Tod whispered, "but they saw me at

the quarries yesterday and . . . one of them fired a gun at me."

Martin's eyes went huge behind his steel-rimmed glasses. "You're an idiot," he said. "Why'd you go up there? They're really dangerous, don't you know that!"

"I wanted to see the foxes," Tod said. His stubborn look had come over his face again. "Anyway, the quarries don't belong to them. I like it up there. You should come up with me. The more other people use the place the less the stupid Breakers can claim it as theirs."

Martin could see the logic of that. "You don't want to get shot, though."

"They missed," Tod said cheerfully. "Shows what bad shots they are. They weren't aiming at me anyway. At least I don't think they were. They were aiming at a fox. And they missed him too!"

"You saw one up there? Was the book any good?"

"It had the coolest thing in it," Tod said. "It tells you how to call foxes to you. I tried it and it worked. It was so cool. Come up with me after school and we'll try it again."

"I don't know if I'll be allowed to," Martin replied. "My mum doesn't like me going out like that. She thinks it's too dangerous."

"So what do you do all the time? Apart from playing the trumpet?"

"Watch TV. Play computer games—I've got some really good ones. You could come over sometime and play them." Martin looked sideways at Tod and said after a slight pause, "Did your sister say anything about me?"

"She said you were a cool dude!"

"No kidding!" Martin went slowly bright red. "She's nice," he said wistfully.

Tod suspected Martin was living in a world of his

own about Charm. The poor guy was doomed to heartbreak.

"Come over to my place after school," Martin suggested. "I'll show you my newest game, and we'll ask my mum about going to the quarries. She might let me go if you tell her about the foxes."

They left school together, going the short way through the top gate and up the street to the railway line. Tod wondered if he would show Martin the fox's grave, but decided against it. He might one day but not yet.

When they came to the end of the street, Martin, who had been describing the new computer game to Tod in detail, stopped in the middle of a *kapow,* and said "Uh-oh," instead. Tod, who had been half listening and half thinking about foxes, looked at him and then followed his gaze.

Up ahead, in the fenced walkway that led to the pedestrian crossing over the train track, were Adrian, his brother, Shaun, and the gang.

Martin walked more slowly. "What are we going to do?" he hissed to Tod.

"Just walk on, I suppose," Tod replied. "They can't do anything to us. Not here. Anyway, Adrian's there too."

Shaun was sitting on the top of the fence. He was wearing his camouflage pants, a black top, sneakers, and a baseball cap back to front. The dark boy with the greyhound face lounged next to him, the green-and-red bandana around his head. The other boy, the stocky one, also in army camouflage, was holding onto Adrian's shoulders. Adrian had his head flung back and his eyes half closed. Tod wondered what part he was acting now. There were two other younger boys that Tod hadn't seen before. One looked quiet and rather dreamy. He was standing at the back of the group, not looking at them, but staring down the railway line. The other was the smallest with reddish hair and freckles. He seemed to be trying to dig up the track with a knife.

Martin walked even more slowly, head down, face turned away, as if not looking at the gang would make them disappear, but Tod studied them all closely. He realized that though he was a bit scared of them he was also intensely interested. His heart was beating a little faster, but it was with excitement as much as fear. Something was going to happen and Adrian knew about it. That was why he had been acting so strangely all day.

"Hi, Adrian," he said boldly as they crossed the railway line toward the boys.

Adrian came dramatically awake. "Tod," he said in a low urgent voice, "this is my brother, Shaun, and he wants to talk to you."

Tod and Martin stopped because they had to. There was no way through the walkway. It was blocked by the gang.

"What about?" Tod said, not the most brilliant response but all he could think of on the spot.

"Lots of things," Shaun said. His voice was just breaking, and it had a strange quality as if he had a slight lisp. "Too many to talk about here." He looked past Tod even though he was speaking to him, and his hands clenched and unclenched the rail along the top of the fence. "Thought you might like to take a train ride with us."

"Sorry," Tod said. "I've got to get home."

"Won't take long," Shaun said. "Just up the track and back. We've got something to show you. Adrian's coming too. No one's going to hurt you."

At that moment the bells began to ring at the level crossing and Tod heard the hoot of a train as it came up the hill.

"There's the train now," the dark boy said. "Let's go."

The one holding Adrian let go of him, and gave Martin a push. "You can shove off," he said. "Go home to Mummy."

"Shall I call the police, Tod?" Martin said bravely.

"Yeah, call the police," Shaun mocked him.

"No, it's okay," Tod said. "I'll be okay. I'll see you later."

There were no barriers or ticket collectors on the platform. Passengers were supposed to use the ticket verifying machines inside the train, but the gang ignored them, and Tod had to as well. The two younger gang members ran up to the front to get the front seat. Adrian and Tod sat a couple of rows behind with the other three. Adrian gave Tod a nudge and winked at him, but didn't say anything. He gazed out of the window while his brother spoke.

"This is Dom," Shaun said, indicating the greyhound boy. "And Justin. The other two up there are Luke and Jamie. You know my name, don't you?"

Tod nodded.

"And you've seen us before, haven't you?"

There didn't seem to be any point in denying it. "I saw you in the quarries, yesterday," Tod said. "You shot at me."

"We weren't shooting at you. You were bloody lucky we didn't hit you. We thought you were a fox," Dom said.

"That's the first thing we want to talk to you about," Shaun said. "You don't go to the quarries. That's our place. I know you're new round here, so maybe you don't understand things yet. I'm being nice to you 'cause you're a mate of Adrian's. I'm explaining things to you carefully. No misunderstandings. Do you get it?"

Tod didn't say anything for a moment. "I'm not hurting you up there," he said finally. "I'll stay away from you. I just want to see the foxes. And I don't want you to shoot them."

"He doesn't get it," Justin said, looking at Shaun.

"You're slow, aren't you?" Shaun said, stumbling more over the *s* sounds as his voice became more threatening. "Adrian said you were slow at schoolwork."

Tod gave Adrian a swift look, but Adrian stared stubbornly out of the window. The train was going slowly up the steep embankment, past the rocks and boulders of the quarry area. Most of them had graffiti tags on them, and there were olive-green spaces on the concrete slabs of the embankment and the sides of the cutting where larger pieces of artwork had been cleaned off and painted over.

"But Adrian says you're good at art," Shaun went on. "He reckons you're really cool at drawing."

"Maybe," Tod said cautiously when there was a silence. "So?"

"I'm an artist too," Shaun said. "I'm a writer. Do you know what that means?"

"You write books?" Tod ventured.

"Huh, wise guy," Dom commented.

"Nah, I do real art graffiti work. And I want to do a real big piece up here. See that space up there?"

He pointed out of the window. Above the railway track ran an older track, perhaps from the days when the quarries were operating. Not much was left of it except the concrete supports, newly cleaned, dull green in the spring sun.

"This is our place," Shaun said again. "I want everyone to know it belongs to the Breakers. If you want to keep coming into our territory, you'll have to be one of us. And the only way to be one of us is to help me paint that big space. You're so good at art, you can help me do it."

He gave Tod a big grin and settled back in his seat.

"It's an honor," Justin told Tod. "Not many people get invited to join, just like that. Even those guys up there," he pointed to Luke and Jamie, "they're not really part of the gang yet."

"They're toys—on probation," Dom added. "Luke racks the materials for us, and Jamie is chalking up his thousand tags."

"Hey, Jamie," Justin called to the red-haired boy. "How many tags you gotta go?"

Jamie turned around and gave them a wicked grin. "Couple of hundred."

"He's okay," Justin said. "Luke's a bit of a wimp, though, aren't you, Luke? Hey, toyboy, aren't you a bit of a wuss?"

"Leave him alone," Shaun said lazily, and then spoke again to Tod. "Are you in or out?"

"I don't know," Tod said. "I'll have to think about it."

"Think about it," Dom exploded, his dark face going darker with anger. "You are slow, aren't you?"

"It's cool," Shaun said. "The kid can think about it. For a couple of minutes. Till we get to Russetdene."

He grinned more widely. He looked quite relaxed, but next to him Justin was seething.

"There's something I don't like about this train," he said, pounding the seat. "Jamie," he shouted again, "do you like this train?"

"I hate it," Jamie said cheerfully.

"So do I. It's too bloody clean."

Tod looked around. The train was one of the new ones, not an old red hen. It looked all right to him. It ran quietly and smoothly, and it was clean and comfortable. There was a sudden change of rhythm and the lights dimmed as the train entered the tunnel.

"One two three go!" Justin shrieked, and chaos erupted.

Jamie had a black marker. He leaped around like a demented imp, tagging the walls and ceiling, wherever he could reach. Then he attacked the seats with his knife. A couple of slashes and they ripped open. The insides burst out.

Justin was also tagging and trashing. The two boys moved like a minicyclone through the carriage. Their timing was perfect. Almost before any of the other passengers—mainly school kids going home and a few elderly people—had time to notice what was happening, let alone protest about it, the train was through the tunnel and stopping at the next station. Justin and Jamie left the train coolly as though they'd had no part in what had taken place.

"Not a clean train now," Dom observed, grinning at Shaun.

Tod was silenced. The attack had been so quick and so pointless. He couldn't understand why anyone would want to do that. He looked from Shaun to Dom and back again. They were both elated, their eyes bright and their cheeks flushed. Adrian had come alive again, and was staring in fascination at the mess. Only Luke, still at the front of the train, seemed to escape the shared excitement. He looked as if he was going to faint. He was shaking, trying to breathe slowly to calm himself down. Tod realized Luke was terrified. He wondered why this boy was part of the gang when he obviously hated what they did. They must have some sort of hold over him. He couldn't imagine what it was.

"Wasn't that fun?" Shaun said.

Tod shook his head. "Not my scene," he replied. He looked at the ripped seats and at the shocked face of the old lady sitting down at the back. She was almost as pale as Luke and she looked as if she was going to cry. She wasn't a tough old bird like Grandma. If Grandma had been on the train she would probably have made a citizen's arrest of Justin and Jamie. This old lady was one of the blue rinse and lavender water sort, and Tod felt kind of responsible and really sorry for her.

It had been flattering and almost exciting to be invited to be part of the gang. No one else had ever asked him to do something like that. Shaun didn't treat him like his family treated him—as someone who needed extra help and had to be looked after all the time. Shaun treated him like an equal. He was actually asking Tod to help him, not the other way around.

He could just see what kind of picture he would have put on the blank space on the side of the hill. And if he was one of the Breakers he could protect Charm, even Martin from them . . . all these thoughts flashed through his head as the train went from Auburn Hills to Tannen. But the other side of the deal was the destructiveness he'd just witnessed, as well as the shooting and the killing in the quarries. He wasn't sure he wanted to be part of that. Shaun had shot the fox. He thought of it now and remembered he had said he would avenge it.

Shaun leaned forward as the train left Tannen. "I really want you to do this, Tod. I don't think you've grasped how much I want you to do it."

Tod could feel the stubborn feeling coming over him. He was rather sorry about it. He knew it was going to cause him a huge amount of trouble. But there didn't seem to be much he could do about it. It felt like the earthy, rocky feeling he'd had when he was in the quarry, as though he was part of the earth and immovable.

"I'm not going to do it," he said. "I don't want to be part of your gang." He could have left it at that, but something else made him say, "I don't like what you do."

He looked Shaun in the eyes for a moment, but didn't like what he saw there. Shaun said nothing, just smiled slightly, and cracked his knuckles in the palm of his other hand.

Tod wasn't sure if he was sorry he'd refused or not. He looked past Shaun to where Luke was still standing with his back to the front window of the train. Luke's mouth was open and he was staring at Tod in amazement. Then he gave him the ghost of a smile. Tod didn't smile back. There was something about Luke that annoyed him. He didn't feel like being friendly with him.

The train stopped at Russetdene. The old lady got out. There was a man in State Transport Authority uniform on the station, surrounded by a group of high school boys. Tod saw the old lady stop to talk to him. She turned and pointed back to the train.

Shaun said, "We'll get off here." He stood up swiftly and ruffled Tod's hair. It seemed like a friendly gesture, but Shaun finished by giving a sharp painful tug.

"I'll ask you again," he said. "You'll change your mind. Keep an eye on him, Adrian. Make sure he gets home. And don't talk to anyone, either of you."

He and Dom swaggered off the train. Luke trailed after them, giving Tod another slight smile as he went past him. Again Tod ignored him. The three boys disappeared into the street.

Adrian spoke to Tod for the first time since they had got on the train. "We'd better get out too. Come on!"

The old lady was still talking to the STA man. The crowd of kids around them had got larger and noisier. The train obviously wasn't going anywhere. The man took out a mobile phone and spoke briefly into it. Then he shouldered his way through the kids and approached the train, just as Adrian and Tod were stepping off onto the platform.

Tod was sure the man was going to stop him and speak to

him. Even though he hadn't done anything wrong he felt horribly guilty. And his eyes were watering from the pain in his head. Adrian was whistling through his teeth. His eyes were bright and his face sunny. He looked like the most innocent person in the world.

The man went straight past them, stood inside the train, and surveyed the damage.

"Don't run," Adrian hissed in Tod's ear, and they walked nonchalantly down the platform and out of the station.

Tod had no idea where they were. He'd never been to this part of the suburbs before.

"How're we going to get home?" he asked Adrian.

"We'll get the bus. But first I've got to get something to eat. I'm starving."

Tod followed him into a snack bar. He was starving too. The smell of roasting chickens and hot chips made him ache all over with hunger. As usual Adrian had plenty of money, and he paid for Tod's chicken and chips as well as his own. Tod had been feeling curiously let down after the tension of the train ride, and the food cheered him up.

"That was cool," Adrian said happily, as they sat at the bus stop, eating. "That's the first time Shaun's let me do anything with them." His voice was full of admiration and pride. "He said I could be in the gang if you join them too."

"I didn't say I would join them!"

Adrian gave Tod a brilliant smile. "But you're going to, aren't you?"

"How come everyone's so sure about that?"

Adrian shrugged. "What else is there to do? It's much easier to be part of them than not. Anyway, Shaun's the coolest person I know. I like doings things with him. Most of the time he tells me to get lost, but he wants you in the gang, so now he wants me too."

He put the last chip in his mouth and wiped his hands on his jeans. "You know why he wants you in the gang? Apart from the art thing, I mean."

Tod shook his head.

"He likes your sister. He wants her to go out with him."

"Charm?" Tod said in surprise. "Your brother likes Charm? She said he was always hassling her."

"That's because he likes her, but she doesn't take any notice of him."

"He hasn't got a chance," Tod said. "She's not interested."

"Well, that's why he was so nice to you."

"Nice to me? He kidnapped me!"

"He did it nicely though. You should have seen how they treated Luke until he agreed to pinch their stuff for them. They gave him hell."

The bus came. Tod got on it thinking about Luke, and how frightened he had looked when the attack was going on. At least he hadn't been frightened. He was feeling quite pleased with himself.

Adrian bought two tickets and they went and sat at the end of the bus.

There were black tags on the seats and the advertisements, but they didn't look familiar.

Adrian followed his gaze. "AWA," he said. "Different posse."

It was a long walk back up the hill from the bus stop, but the chicken and chips had restored the boys' energy and they were still hyped up from the train trip. They chased each other up the street, making rude gestures and shouting at cars that went past. Halfway up Adrian slipped into a Three Musketeers role and started declaiming *all for one and one for all* in a French accent. It started to rain heavily, though, as they went past the school, dampening their spirits a little. They slapped palms to say good-bye, Adrian switching roles skillfully to American street kid. He cut through the school grounds to his house on the other side of the oval. Tod went by the top street: it was too late and too dark to go through the reserve.

The spiny plants waved their strange leaves at him as he came up to Grandma's house. The lights were on inside and it looked welcoming and safe. He could smell cooking. He went into the kitchen, thinking happily how much he liked Dallas, but she greeted him with a scolding.

"Toddy, where've you been? It's so late. I was starting to get worried about you."

"I was out with Adrian," he said, annoyed at having to explain everything to her all the time. "We took the train, and then we had to get the bus back."

"I was afraid you'd got lost," she said. "I thought you might be in the quarries. You could fall up there and no one would know where to find you."

"I wasn't up there today," he said impatiently. "Anyway, I wouldn't fall." More to change the subject than anything else he said, "Where's Mum?"

"She had to go out. She's got a gig at a club." Dallas was frowning. "So much for wanting us all to eat together as a family! But she's going to phone when she gets there to make sure you're back. And a friend of yours called—in fact he's called every half hour since I got home. You'd better ring him now. It's Martin and the number's on the pad."

Tod went to use the phone before she could tell him off any more.

"I was getting ready to call the police!" Martin said. Tod had to reassure him over and over again that he was fine, and that Martin shouldn't tell his parents.

The phone was in the hallway, on a little table. There was nowhere to sit and the wind whistled under the front door. It was uncomfortable and cold standing there, so Tod didn't want to talk for long. He told Martin he'd fill him in on all the details in the morning at school, and Martin said he'd ask if he could go to the quarries. When Tod put the phone down he had a sudden flash of Luke's face. It made him realize that Luke and Martin both had the same look. It was that look of fear that made other people pick on them. But he didn't have that look. Shaun had proved that, by asking for his help. Of course, he'd said he wasn't going to join the Breakers but he had to admit being asked had made him feel proud.

He ate a large helping of stew followed by one of Grandma's apple crumbles. She and Dallas were getting on like a house on fire, cooking together, swapping recipes. Charm said very little, and didn't eat much. Tod found himself studying her. It was surprising that suddenly everyone seemed to be falling for her, but then, as he'd noticed the day before, she had suddenly started to look stunning. He felt saddened by it as though she were disappearing from him, heading out over some uncharted sea while he was still standing on the shore.

The phone rang when he was eating apple crumble. It was Leonie. Tod reassured her that he was fine, and promised to tell her next time he was going to be late. He could hear the background noise of the club, the buzz of voices and laughter.

"How's it going?" he said.

"I'm as nervous as anything. There's a huge crowd!" But Leonie didn't sound nervous so much as excited and happy. He wished her luck and went back and finished his dessert.

He went to bed and thought about the day. The wind was howling outside the little lean-to, and he could hear rain spattering on the tin roof. It was a bit like sleeping in a caravan. He hadn't liked the room when they'd first moved to Grandma's but now he did. He yawned and stretched comfortably.

He thought about the quarry and what it would be like to camp up there. He wondered what the foxes were doing that night. Would they be undercover somewhere, snug and warm in a den, or would they be out in the rain, cold and hungry, looking for something to eat?

He didn't want to talk to his family about Shaun and the gang. He felt it was stuff they wouldn't understand. If his dad had been there he might have been able to tell him. Perhaps he would write to him. If only writing letters wasn't so hard. Perhaps he could phone him . . . but Grandma had gone on and on about the last phone bill. . . .

Just before he fell asleep he remembered the flames of the campfire in the quarry. They flickered behind his closed eyelids, and turned into the colors of his dreams.

SIX

The next day was fresh and sweet smelling after the rain. The air was still cold, but the sun came out in the afternoon, making the asphalt on the road and the playground steam. Tod went to Martin's place after school. The house was across the main road and further down the hill, and the suburb felt different from where Tod lived. It was more of a typical suburb—cozy, safe, and a bit tame—not almost real bush like up at Grandma's. It was further away from the railway too, and you couldn't hear the trains or the level crossing bells.

Martin's mother was home, and she was so pleased to see Tod it gave him the idea that perhaps Martin didn't bring many friends back to his place. She made them a big snack for afternoon tea—peanut butter sandwiches and homemade cake with flavored milk to drink—and then they played Martin's new computer game for a little while. Martin was so skillful at it, Tod felt slow and clumsy next to him and, though the game was ingenious and colorful, he knew he wasn't getting involved in it in the way Martin did. He found he was just a bit scornful of it because no matter how clever it was, it wasn't real.

He was impatient too, because he wanted to get to the quarries before it got too late, and time was running out.

When they finally got Martin's mum's permission to go and had promised her they would be back before dark, they had barely an hour to get up there and back.

"Let's run!" Tod said, and they jogged up the hill, through the school grounds, past Tod's house, and over the railway line.

In the lane Martin slowed to a walk, holding his side and panting.

"Got a stitch," he explained.

Down the hill the bells were ringing for the 5:01 to the city. "If we don't hurry, we may as well go back now," Tod grumbled. "We'll never have time to get up to the quarries and back, and then your mum'll freak."

At the top of the lane Martin peered through the gloom down into the gully. "Do you think there's anyone there?" he said nervously.

"I don't know," Tod said. He was feeling a bit apprehensive too and it was making him snappy. "Come on!"

He jumped down the steep slope and looked back up at Martin.

"It's getting dark," Martin said, hesitantly. "I really think I'd better get home. We did promise my mum we'd be back before it got dark."

"I'll show you where the fox drinks," Tod pleaded.

"We can go back to my place and play my computer game again," Martin replied.

Tod looked at him for a moment. Perhaps they should leave the exploring till the weekend. But then the stubborn earthy feeling took hold of him. He wanted to call the fox again and he wanted to go back to the mysterious dark quarry. He didn't want to be bothered with Martin's mum worrying about them. It made him feel like a little kid. He compared Martin scornfully with the Breakers. He couldn't imagine any of them hesitating as Martin was now . . . except Luke of course.

He gave Martin a kind of wave with his hand, which could have meant either *see you,* or *get lost you're a deadbeat.* Then without looking back he loped over the creek and up past the bank.

The wind of the night before had dropped and it hadn't rained all day, but the ground was still wet and the trees and shrubs were damp. The mud was sticky red, and before long his shoes were caked in it. A couple of times he slipped and fell forward onto his hands. The mud squelched between his fingers, cool and malleable. He wiped his hands on his jeans where the mud left red streaks.

He moved quietly, ears straining to hear any sign of the gang, but all he could hear were the birds and the chattering of the creek alongside him. He stopped at the pool in the creek and, because his hands were dirty, he didn't put his fingers in the water. He dropped down on all fours and lapped briefly from it.

When he got to the clearing at the top of the hill he stopped to catch his breath and think about what he would do. He had thought he would hide and call the fox again—but the main reason for coming up this evening had been to show Martin. Now Martin wasn't here, he wasn't sure what to do. He looked around, wondering whether to go home now before it got too late, wishing Martin had come with him, angry with him for not being there.

He didn't have to call the fox. It was already there, waiting for him. He saw it beyond the olive bushes, watching him, motionless. Their eyes met briefly. The fox turned. He caught a glimpse of the white-tipped brush as he dived into the thicket of branches to follow it.

He scrambled up the hill as he'd done before when he'd thought the gang was after him. He lost sight of the fox almost immediately, but in spite of the growing darkness he found the way easily, as if he were being led. He went on all fours. The track was damp and soft under his fingers, though occasionally he slipped on sharp, reddish stones. The branches of the olives scratched at him as he slipped through them, but they could not slow him down.

The olives gave way to the ash trees and he could stand again. He looked back down the hill. Beyond the gray-green tangle of olive leaves he could just see the sea in the distance. It was still light, but ahead of him it was much darker—the mysterious darkness that both attracted him and scared him.

I'll just go and explore the quarry, he thought. Just see what's up there. Then I'll go home.

As he went under the ash trees and through the darkness, he caught a whiff of the strong smell of fox. His hearing sharpened so he thought he could understand what the birds were saying. He swung his head from side to side and his step lightened until he was moving soundlessly. When he came to the rock wall he dropped on all fours again and wriggled through the tunnel.

Out in the quarry on the other side it was lighter. The sun fell on the highest part of the rock face giving the ancient strata a glowing apricot warmth. Where the earth had been cut open its shape was exposed like bones. It made Tod feel very strange looking right into the earth like that, as though he were in a sacred place, seeing things he was not supposed to see.

The quarry was beautiful and ugly at the same time. It was clear how the work on it all those years ago had wrecked the original landscape. Once, where he was standing would have been underground. Who knew what people and animals would have lived above his head? And what trees would have grown there before they were overtaken and strangled by the olive and the ash, by boneweed and brambles, and all the other introduced plants?

The floor of the quarry was covered in shaley pieces of rock, between huge boulders that had fallen from the cliffs. Here and there the floor was smoother with a mat of tough, reddish grass.

Tod stood still for a few moments, sniffing the air and listening intently. He kept thinking he could see things moving out of the corner of his eye, but when he spun to look at them directly there was nothing there. Sometimes he thought he saw people, sometimes animals, but then he convinced himself it was just the trees and the grass moving. He began to walk slowly around the edge of the quarry, up against the rocks, working his way stealthily toward where he had seen the fire.

There was no sign of any fire and no smell of smoke—no smell of humans at all, apart from his own, largely covered with mud, but soon Tod realized he was following the scent of the fox. It led him around the side of the quarry to a flat place encircled by rocks. The floor was soft and sandy, and it was warm out of the wind. Tod crouched behind one of the rocks and peered into the circle. Under one huge boulder was a cave. Someone or something had piled olive branches across its entrance to hide it and to give more shelter. The sand in front had a smooth look as though the same something sat or lay there and, in front of the smooth sand, was a little circle of stones, blackened at the inner edge, containing the dead remains of a fire. Around the fire were bones and bits of fur.

Tod sniffed again. He could smell the bones—they made

him hungry—and there was also a very slight smell of humans here, sort of humans mixed with fox. He was puzzled. He'd thought he was going to find the fox's den—and the cave in the rocks did look just like a den. But even the smartest fox couldn't make a fire. And surely a smart fox wouldn't have its den anywhere near where humans hung out.

He stepped forward, skin prickling, and tiptoed to the cave. His new sharp hearing could detect not the slightest movement. There was no one there, but there were signs of someone's camp. Branches had been cut and laid to make a bed, and there was a rough blanket that looked like fur thrown over it. At the entrance was a very sharp-looking knife with a bone handle and an iron pot with a bone spoon in it.

Disappointment stabbed Tod sharply. He'd wanted to see the fox, not someone's camp. He'd thought he'd found a secret place that no one else knew about, but someone else did know about it already, and had made their home in it. It was their place, not his. It was probably one of the unemployed, homeless vagrants Grandma had been telling him about. They lived in the reserves because they had nowhere else to go. Getting to be as bad as the Depression, Grandma said, when she was a girl and strings of men used to trail past the farm, looking for food, shelter, and work.

It might even be the Breakers' hideout. He'd been mad to think he could find a place around here that no one else knew about. It was practically in the suburbs for heaven's sake. He'd been acting like an idiot, thinking he was out in the wilds.

He felt again as if something were watching him. He could feel eyes on him. He slipped back into the shelter of the rocks, but he couldn't see or hear anything. A tremendous uneasiness took hold of him. He wanted to get out of there quickly. It was too lonely and too strange. And he was hungry, with a deep gnawing hunger he'd never felt before. He had an image of the kitchen at home and the idea of food made his mouth water.

He left the quarry as silently as he'd entered it and trotted swiftly home.

Tod was tired that night and didn't feel like playing cards with Grandma or talking to anyone. He went to bed early. When he went into his little room he was delighted to see Grandma's big black-and-white cat curled up on his bed.

"Hello, Inkspot," he said softly, standing by the door, not moving in case the cat should take fright and run away. He willed it to stay.

Inkspot opened one eye, then closed it again. He stretched one leg a little, showing his claws, and relaxed deeper into the old satiny eiderdown that covered Tod's bed.

Tod went up to the bed and very gently stroked the cat behind the ears. He could hear a faint rusty sound. Inkspot was purring.

Tod sat down next to him. He went on stroking him for a long time, feeling tireder and tireder. He was just about to get up and put his pajamas on when the door burst open and Charm rushed into the room.

Inkspot opened his eyes in alarm, leaped in the air, and disappeared under the bed.

"You idiot," Tod yelled. "He was just getting used to me!"

"Oh, sorry, Toddy," she groaned. "I didn't know he was in here, did I?"

"You should knock before you come in," Tod said. "You always tell me to."

"Sorry again." Charm grinned at him. "And that's two apologies you've got from me so don't expect another one."

She dropped down on the bed where Inkspot had been sitting.

"So what do you want? I'm going to bed," Tod said. He felt as if he could fall asleep on his feet. He couldn't wait to slide into bed and close his eyes. He was sure he'd never been as tired as this in his whole life.

"Just wanted to talk to someone. Mum's out again and Dallas and Grandma have covered recipes and gone on to knitting. I worry about that girl, Tod. She's going to be middle-aged before she's even grown up."

Tod laughed. He hadn't thought of Dallas like that before, but Charm was right. "Oh well, if she takes up knitting she'll probably knit something cool for you."

"Yeah, I know, I know. I don't really want to change her. She's okay." Charm stretched out on the bed and yawned. "Anyway, you can't change people, can you? Not really."

Tod shrugged. He caught the yawn and yawned hugely too. There were a few seconds of silence and then Charm said abruptly, "What do you think of Shaun?"

Since Tod had been thinking about him on and off all day the mention of Shaun's name made him start.

"Shaun who?" he said guardedly.

"Shaun Stone. He said he knew you."

"I don't really know him," Tod replied. "I know his brother, Adrian. We're in the same class at school . . ." He thought, I could tell Charm about the train ride. I could talk to her about it. But he wasn't sure.

"And?" Charm prompted him.

"And what?"

"I thought you were going to say something else."

Tod shook his head.

"The girls think he's really good-looking," Charm said. "Do you?"

"He's okay."

Tod lay back on the pillow and thought for a few seconds. "Do you like him, then?"

"No, not really." Charm tried to sound casual, but she gave Tod a swift look from under her long black lashes. "Someone told me today that he likes me."

"Who told you?"

"One of the boys he hangs around with—Dom, I think he's called—told one of the girls in my English class to tell me."

"So what did you tell her to tell Dom to say back?" Tod couldn't believe he was having this conversation with Charm, who was usually so secretive. He was enjoying it.

"I said I'd talk to him tomorrow."

"So do you like him?"

Charm didn't say anything for a while. Her eyes had a strange intense look. Finally she said, "I don't know yet." She laughed to break the tension. "He's kind of attractive in a weird way."

"Not just weird?"

"You don't understand, Toddy. I like him and I don't like him at the same time. It's such a strange feeling."

"Do you think he's a bit dangerous?" He knew what Charm meant. Shaun both attracted and scared him.

Charm grinned at him. "At least he's not boring." She sat up and stretched her arms above her head. "Oh well, I'm off to bed." She looked round the little lean-to, with its faded brown carpet and orange curtains that clashed with the old pink eiderdown. "You're so lucky having your own room. I wish I could sleep out here."

"Well, I'm not sharing with Dallas," Tod said firmly.

"Sweet dreams," Charm said as she left the room.

Tod tore off his clothes, threw on his pajamas, and

switched out the light. He was too tired even to brush his teeth. He made his way into bed in the dark. Just as he was about to fall asleep he felt something jump on him. He smiled as he realized it was Inkspot. Sleepily he put his hand out and rubbed the old cat behind the ears. Then he fell into a deep and dreamless sleep.

It seemed only seconds later that he opened his eyes, but the whole night had passed, and it was light in his room. Inkspot was meowing at the door. Tod got up to let him out. Then Inkspot ran to the back door and waited expectantly. Tod opened the door and looked out into the backyard.

Up the hill, outside the hen run, a fox was sniffing around the wire. When it heard the door open it flung up its head and stared in the direction of the house. Tod shouted at it and ran up the steps. The ground under his bare feet was damp and freezing. The fox flattened itself against the grass, wove like a snake to the back of the yard, slipped under the fence, and disappeared.

There was no sound from the poultry—none of the clucking and quacking that usually started up as soon as anyone opened the back door. Tod tore on up the hill and looked in the run. Two of the white hens lay unmoving on the dirt. The other hens, the bantams, and the ducks sat huddled in a corner. They looked as if they were in shock. They didn't move or make a sound. Tod hurtled back down the hill shouting out, "Grandma! Grandma! Wake up!"

He hammered on her door and heard her grumbling inside. She opened the door and peered out at him with half-awake eyes. She was wearing blue striped men's pajamas and her short gray hair was standing on end.

"Crikey, boy, what's the matter? I was sleeping that

soundly. What's happened? Is the house on fire?"

"There was a fox in the yard," he said breathlessly. "And two of the chooks aren't getting up!"

She swore under her breath and grabbed her dressing gown from the end of the bed. Following Tod through the laundry she pulled on her gumboots. They both hurried up the steps. The hens began to cluck softly when they saw Grandma.

"There, there," she said in a crooning voice. "You poor old things had a bit of a scare. I might have known it—I slept so deeply. Deep sleep, fox sleep."

"What do you mean?" Tod said.

"Every time there's a fox attack on the poultry, I never hear it. It's like the fox runs around the house and puts a spell on you to sleep. They're devils, all right. I know you like 'em, Toddy, and they're beautiful animals—but you should see what they can do to a shed full of chooks. It's wicked."

She opened the door of the run as she spoke and stepped inside. "Lucky this fellow didn't get in," she said. "We fooled him this time."

"Didn't he get those two?" Tod said, following her in. He knelt down beside the two seemingly lifeless hens and stroked one's head. To his amazement its eyes snapped open and it gave a faint squawk. Grandma picked up the other one, and scratched its back between its wings. It drew its feet up under it convulsively. It was alive too.

"They'll be all right," she said with relief. "I've seen it happen before. The old chooks get so scared they sort of faint with fright. You think they're dead, and then all of a sudden they get up and walk away."

"Did the fox put a spell on them too?" Tod asked.

"I wouldn't put it past the devil," Grandma said. She put the chook down and it scrabbled to its feet and started pecking at the dirt. The other poultry seemed to unfreeze slowly too. They moved out of their huddle and began to cluck and quack.

Grandma stepped outside the run again and went all round checking it. "Look, Tod," she called. "He tried to dig under the wire here. No wonder they were all in a panic. He must have been here for quite a while."

Tod went outside, closing the door carefully, and crouched down beside his grandmother. There was a large hole in the earth along one side of the run. He could see the scrape marks from the fox's claws. But the wire had been dug well into the ground and secured with rocks. This time the fox hadn't been able to break through.

"We'll have to do some more work on it," Grandma said. "You can help me after school, all right?"

"Sure," Tod said. He was feeling slightly guilty. He'd called the fox, after all. Perhaps it had followed him and found the chooks. What if it had killed them? He was so glad they were all still alive.

"You're very quiet," Grandma said. "It's all right. The chooks are all okay. And the ducks. No one got hurt this time."

"I thought it might be my fault," he said slowly.

"Is it your fault foxes kill to eat? The foxes were around here before you started being interested in them. No, it's no one's fault. It's just the way things are. If people didn't keep poultry penned up the foxes wouldn't kill as many. The ducks would be on the water where the fox can't reach them, and the chooks would be up a tree. You can't blame the old fox. It's just his nature. Doesn't stop me getting mad at the devils, all the same."

She finished her inspection of the run and straightened

up. "Got out of bed too fast," she grumbled, rubbing the base of her spine. "I need time to get the stiffness out of my joints in the morning. Come in, boy, let's go and get a cuppa."

Charm was in the kitchen, sitting at the table, a mug of coffee in her hands.

"You're up early," Grandma said in surprise. "Not like you to be up at this hour."

"Tod woke me up yelling," Charm mumbled. "And I had the weirdest night. I thought I was awake all night, but I must have been asleep and dreaming. I could hear all these strange things going on but I couldn't open my eyes and wake up."

When she looked up at Tod he was amazed at the huge rings under her eyes. She looked as if she hadn't slept for a week. "Didn't you hear the alarm?" she went on, rubbing her eyes. Her hair was all over her face.

"Didn't hear a thing all night," Grandma replied.

"*You have violated a protected area. The police were called. Leave immediately,*" Charm droned. "On and on all night. I've got the bloody thing on the brain. Didn't you hear it, Toddy?"

He shook his head. "It was the foxspell," he replied. "The fox made us all sleep really deeply."

Charm gave him a cynical look. "Oh yeah? Grandma been telling you fairy tales again? He's too old for that sort of crap," she told Grandma. "He'll be in high school next year. You can't fill his head up with nonsense."

Grandma was offended. She didn't say anything to Charm, but her face went stiff and cross and she made a cup of tea with jerky movements, spilling the water as she poured it into the pot.

"Why don't you use the tea bags Mum bought?" Charm said.

"Why don't you hold your tongue, girl?" Grandma snapped back. "I've been making tea for sixty odd years and I'll make it the way I like."

Charm didn't reply. She took another swig of coffee from her mug. "I'm sure there was someone outside too," she said. "I kept hearing things. I kept hearing slashing and cutting, like there were people outside with swords."

"Now who's talking nonsense?" Grandma demanded. "You must have been dreaming." She took a large gulp of tea and sighed deeply.

They heard the alarm ring from the girls' room and the sounds of Dallas getting out of bed. Tod yawned. The deep sleep had made him dopey and slow. "I suppose I'd better get dressed," he said. He was going to the bathroom when he heard a meowing from outside the front door. He went to let Inkspot in.

As he opened the door he smelled a strong, sharp smell like fresh cut grass but much, much stronger, how blood would smell if it were green. He looked out into the gray morning. There was too much light on the steps. Immediately he saw why.

The huge plants had been savagely attacked. Their spearlike leaves lay all over the pathway. Someone had hacked them to pieces. And on the pathway, visible under the leaves, and on the gateposts were fresh black graffiti tags.

"Jeez." Charm had come up behind Tod and was leaning in the doorway. Inkspot leaped past her meowing crossly. "See! I wasn't dreaming. Someone *was* out slashing and cutting with swords."

SEVEN

Grandma called the police. She was more distraught than Tod had ever seen her.

"Those plants were there when Ken and I bought the house," she lamented. "They're forty years old or more."

"Let's face it, Ma, they were pretty ugly," said Leonie, who had been woken up by all the noise and was drifting around in her rose-pink kimono. "We can put something else in—something prettier."

"They might grow back," Dallas comforted Grandma. "We can tidy up the damage and they'll probably come good again."

"Look at the mess they made of them," Grandma said. "And all that graffiti muck! Who'd want to do something like that? And what have we ever done to upset anyone?"

Tod thought about the ways he had been upsetting the Breakers. Their revenge had been swift and unexpected. Also he was surprised by his own reaction. He was really shocked, and sorry for poor old Grandma, but he was strangely excited as well. His mother was right, the plants had been ugly. He hadn't liked them at all. He couldn't really blame anyone for slashing them to bits. And as for the graffiti—just Jamie notching up his tags, he found himself thinking, as though he were seeing things from a different point of view.

When the police came they told the family the depot had also been broken into in the night.

"I heard the alarm," Charm said, but everyone else had been deep asleep.

"Ferocious-looking plants," observed the younger policeman. He had a close-cropped bullet head, and a big mouth and nose. His gray eyes were creased at the edges as if he were laughing at some private joke. He sounded as if he were laughing now at the plants. "Do you reckon they fought back? Our suspect's probably covered in slashes."

"Got any idea who it might have been?" the older man asked, pushing up his horn-rimmed glasses and rubbing the bridge of his nose. His hair was receding and he looked weary. "Any enemies around here? Any feuds with neighbors, that sort of thing?"

"Certainly not!" Grandma replied indignantly. "I've never had a feud with anyone in my life. And I've lived in this house for forty years and never had so much as a cross word with my neighbors."

"What about you kids?" said Bullet Head. "You met up with any of the local gangs?"

Tod felt Charm's eyes on him. He glanced at her furtively. She shook her head very slightly. He was sure Bullet Head would have noticed.

"They don't have anything to do with gangs and that sort of thing," Leonie leaped to her children's defense. "Just because you think we look a bit weird," she said to Horn Rims. "You've got no right accusing my kids."

He looked wearier than ever. "Did I accuse anyone of anything?" he said, spreading out his hands in a placating gesture.

"And who thinks you look weird?" said Bullet Head, giving

Leonie an admiring stare. He turned his attention back to Tod and Charm. "You know anything about anything?"

Tod didn't want to open his mouth. He was quite alarmed by being so close to policemen. He felt as if they could look right inside his head and see all the things he'd been doing. He wondered if they knew about the train ride too. He didn't dare say anything in case he said too much.

"Tod, if you know who it was you should tell the police," Dallas said sharply.

"I don't know who it was," he replied.

"Have you met up with the mob that call themselves the Breakers?" Bullet Head said. Hearing the name made Tod jump.

"Not really," he muttered.

"We think these could be their tags," the policeman went on.

"If you know who it is you can deal with them then," Grandma said eagerly.

Bullet Head and Horn Rims exchanged a look that said things weren't that simple.

"We'll do what we can," Horn Rims promised. "There's a couple of lads we'll go and check up on."

Bullet Head didn't look very taken by the idea. As the two policemen left down the steps, he picked up one of the slashed-off leaves and pretended to stab his partner with it. They could hear him laughing all the way to the car.

After the police had gone Grandma and Leonie started clearing up the plants, and Dallas and Charm left for the high school. Tod walked slowly down to the primary school. He had so much to think about he wasn't sure how he was going to cope with school. He didn't seem to be learning anything there anyway. Ms. Linkman was too busy to spend much time with him and he knew he was slipping further and further behind the rest of the class.

When he came out of the reserve he realized it was much later than he had thought. There were no kids around outside the school and the crossing lights were off. The siren must have gone already which meant he was late. He didn't feel like going to the office to explain why, and almost without noticing what he was doing he turned around and began walking back through the reserve.

At the railway line he began to trot. There were some workmen in the depot yard, scrubbing graffiti off a couple of trucks. Tod didn't want them to see him, so he followed the train track up the hill, without crossing it, keeping low and weaving from bush to bush. When the yard was hidden by the cutting he crossed the track and worked his way upward toward the quarry.

He moved lightly and surely, making no sound as he padded up the hill. He found he was turning his head slightly from side to side all the time, watching for flickers of movement. And his sense of smell was becoming more and more acute. He knew a cat had been up the track in the night, and a human had walked a dog there in the morning. The different odors from the dump mingled with the earth and the gum trees, and a sort of spicy smell like cough mixture from one of the shrubs made his nose tingle. The smells made him hungry.

He was panting a little from the steepness of the track when he got to the top of the hill. There was a small grassed area where rabbits came to feed in the early morning. Tod could smell where they had been and his stomach growled. The sun was warm on his back now, delightfully warm after the chill under the trees. He squatted down and turned his face toward it, closing his eyes and seeing red patterns behind his lids. They reminded him of the fire in the quarry.

When he opened his eyes he saw a snake lying in a little hollow a couple of yards away. He couldn't help jumping with surprise before he realized it was not a live snake, but an empty skin. He walked over to inspect it. It was pale brown and scaly, almost perfect as though the snake had just crawled out of it. There was a dry rustling sound when he touched it with his hand. It made him feel strange looking at it. The snake had shed its skin, as snakes did every year and had done for . . . how many thousand years would it be? Maybe even a million years. The earth had existed for millions of years, long before people evolved. He had seen its ancient bones in the quarry.

For millions of years the earth had been spinning, turning every day to meet the sun again, supporting its cargo of plant and animal life. No matter what humans were doing or worrying about or scheming, the earth went on with its business of supporting life, and life went on doing what it always did.

He felt again as if the human world were slipping away from him and as if he were becoming part of the earth. School seemed distant and meaningless. He could hardly remember what he went there for.

The rumble of traffic reminded him where he was. On the other side of the gully, cars followed the main road down toward the city. He could see a bus, then a truck. He wondered if anyone driving down could see him. He left the snake skin where it lay and drew back a little into the shelter of the olive bushes. From there the skin turned back into a live snake.

Deciding he would make this his base he took his school-bag off his back. He opened it to see if there was any food and found the lunch Dallas had made for him. A peanut-butter-and-honey sandwich, a piece of chocolate cake, an apple, and a bottle of water. He took a mouthful of water and ate half the piece of cake. He was wrapping it up to put it away for later when he froze. His sharp hearing had caught a sound—a twig snapping or a stone being displaced. Someone was coming up the hill. He slid quickly further back under the roots of the olives, flattening himself against the ground, swinging his head and sniffing the air.

He noted that the human had the wind behind him. He caught his scent. Tod grinned when he realized he knew who it was. A couple of moments later Adrian came half running, half stumbling up the hill.

He stopped at the top, holding his hand to his side as if he had a stitch, breathing heavily. Then like Tod he caught sight of the snakeskin and leaped backward with a squeal. After squinting at the skin for a few moments he picked up a stick and poked at it cautiously, keeping a safe distance.

Tod wriggled out of his hiding place and came silently up on him from behind. He touched him on the leg and hissed.

Adrian dropped the stick and shot forward, jumping clear over the snake skin and nearly falling down the hill. When he saw it was Tod he yelled at him.

"For heaven's sake you nearly gave me a heart attack. What are you doing up here?" Then he threw himself on Tod.

At first Tod thought it was a play fight. He went on pretending to be a snake, hissing and striking with his hand when he could get it free. But after a few quite hefty thumps from Adrian he realized that for Adrian it was not a play fight. It was a real one.

"Hey," he called out, after getting a fist in his eye that made it sting and water. "Watch it. That hurt!"

"It's meant to hurt, you bastard," Adrian muttered through his teeth.

Tod managed to get on top and pin Adrian down. Adrian was much lighter and when Tod was sitting on him he couldn't move.

"What's the problem?" Tod said. "I was just joking about the snake. Did you think it was alive?"

"It's not the snake, you idiot." Adrian's face was pale and his eyes red rimmed as if he had been crying. "It's you. You went to the police, didn't you? You told them about Shaun." He wriggled and jerked under Tod's hands.

"I didn't go to the police," Tod said, gripping tighter. "They came to our house because someone chopped up Grandma's plants and sprayed graffiti all over the path. Grandma called them."

"So who gave them Shaun's name? They turned up at our house looking for him just now."

"I didn't tell them," Tod said. "They knew about the Breakers already. They asked if I knew them, but I said I didn't. And no one mentioned Shaun. They just said they had some lads to talk to. Did they talk to him?"

"No, he didn't come home last night. Mum didn't know where he was. So she went off her face at the police." Adrian wriggled even more violently. "Something's sticking into my back," he complained. "Let me up."

"No more fighting," Tod said, not moving.

"Okay, okay," Adrian mumbled. Tod got off him and he sat up and rubbed the leaves off his back. "Why aren't you at school?" he said, looking suspiciously at Tod.

"Why aren't you?" Tod countered.

"I wanted to find Shaun and tell him what the police said. I went to the high school but he wasn't around. I thought he might have come up here. I didn't know I was going to run into you—the traitor himself," he added dramatically.

"I'm not a traitor," Tod cried out. "I wouldn't do that!"

"You told him you wouldn't join the gang," Adrian said. "Then your house gets attacked and the police turn up at our house. What am I supposed to think?"

Tod couldn't work out what he was thinking himself, let alone analyze Adrian's thoughts. He kicked at the broken bits of snakeskin at their feet. He had a sudden picture in his mind of the fox in the yard. He remembered the deep fox sleep of the night before and yawned. The sun was getting warmer and warmer and it was making him sleepy. It was very bright and he was longing to find somewhere dark and shady to doze till evening . . . he shook himself. He never slept in the daytime. What was he thinking of?

"You want to look around a bit?" Adrian was saying. "We might find Shaun up here."

"Are you sure you want to hang out with me?" Tod said, sarcastically. "You said I was a traitor, remember?"

Adrian shrugged. He seemed to have forgiven Tod. "Let's stay up here all day," he said. "Have you got anything to eat? We can make a camp somewhere. We could come here every day instead of school." He walked across to the olive bush where Tod had left his schoolbag and dropped on hands and knees to look inside it, a pathetic starving expression on his face. Tod couldn't help laughing. He joined him under the bush and they shared the sandwich and the remains of the cake. Then they drank most of the water.

The dead leaves under them were dry and slippery. Adrian stretched gingerly out on them and yawned. "Beats school any day," he mumbled. "Wonder what Linkman's doing now."

"Telling everyone to be helpful and cooperative."

"Grumbling 'cause she's got to teach thirty-two kids."

"We're doing her a favor," Tod said cheerfully. "She'll only have thirty today!"

"Yeah, they should encourage us to cut school. Gives the teachers a break."

They lay there in silence for a while. Tod could feel sleepiness creeping over him, a light dozing, in which he was fully aware of every changing sound around him, and yet he was sleeping. He had to be sleeping because he was dreaming. He was running fast on all fours across a stretch of hillside, and he could feel the power of the earth coming through each foot with every step he took. It was the power of the earth that fed and sustained him, and he was part of it. It flowed into him and made him what he was. He dozed and dreamed, and in the middle of the dream a sound hit his ears and, without thinking, almost without waking, he rose silently and began to snake his way swiftly up the side of the hill.

"Hey!" Adrian said behind him. "Hey, Tod. Where you off to? Wait for me."

The voice woke him more fully. "Someone's coming," he turned to hiss to Adrian, and then went on with his soundless flight, Adrian crashing through the bushes after him.

Tod was using the fox trail he'd followed before, picking up the scent, noticing landmarks and signs almost unconsciously. But when he came through the olive trees he realized he was disoriented. There were no huge ash trees up here. And though there were rocks and boulders in front of him, cast about as he might he could not find the fox tunnel. The rocks were right up against the retaining wall and above his head the traffic roared relentlessly up and down the steep twisty road. When he had run up here before, following the big fox, he had never been aware of either the traffic or the road. Their presence now unnerved him.

Adrian didn't notice anything was wrong. He was looking out over the gully toward the sea. "There is someone down there," he said. "Look!"

Following his pointing finger, Tod could see a tiny figure below. Even at that distance he could recognize the black hair and the skinny shape. It was Charm.

Adrian said something which a truck overhead drowned out completely. Tod was about to shout "What?! when he caught another flicker of movement below him. Someone else came out through the bushes and as Charm turned to face whoever it was, Adrian exclaimed, "Jeez, it's Shaun!"

They could watch the action below as though it were a puppet play. They saw Shaun grab Charm's hand, and saw her pull away after a second. They saw both sit down on the grass. Shaun was digging stones out of the earth and chucking them down the hill. They could catch the sound of voices, but they were too distant to hear the words.

"Woo!" Adrian said quietly. "A lovers' meeting!"

Charm lay down on her back, her arm over her face, shielding her eyes from the sun. Shaun leant over her, but she pushed him off and jumped to her feet. Tod knew she was angry by the way she stood. She was yelling something at Shaun—they could hear the voice much more clearly. Then she walked abruptly away and they lost sight of her among the olive trees.

"Aww!" Adrian exclaimed, disappointed.

Shaun didn't follow her. He sat with his knees drawn up under his chin, staring out over the trees to the city. After a few moments he took out a cigarette and lit it.

"Let's go down," Adrian said. "I want to talk to him."

Tod wasn't sure he wanted to talk to Shaun at all, but it

seemed cowardly to skulk up there while Adrian went down. After all he would have to face Shaun sooner or later, and it might be better to do it with Adrian there. So he followed Adrian down the steep slope, slipping and sliding at his heels, until they both came down at a run out into the spot where Shaun was sitting.

"Hey, Shaun!" Adrian said. "The cops are looking for you."

Shaun didn't reply, just looked them both up and down, with narrowed eyes, grinning slightly.

"Where did you go last night?" Adrian demanded.

"None of your business," Shaun said lazily, leaning back and taking a deep drag at his cigarette. Tod noticed his hand was deeply scratched in several places. He knew it had been Shaun slashing the plants. He felt Shaun's eyes on him. Shaun knew he knew—and he wasn't in the least bit bothered by it.

In fact he was grinning more broadly.

"Don't laugh," Tod said angrily. "It wasn't funny what you did. My grandma was upset."

"My grandma was upset," Shaun mocked him. He sat up quickly and threw the cigarette butt away behind him.

"You know what you can do about it, you've been told before. You can join us and help us. There are a lot of things you can help us with. And you can stop hanging around this place spying on me."

"I'm not spying on you!" Tod returned. "I'm not interested in you."

"He's interested in foxes, Shaun," Adrian put in helpfully.

"It would be more sensible if he was interested in me," Shaun said. "I could be a lot more important to him than foxes. But if you're that keen on foxes, mate, I'll tell you what we'll do. Next time we see you up here, you can be the fox. And we'll hunt you just like we hunt the fox, and if we see you we shoot . . ." He let his voice trail away menacingly and took another cigarette from the packet. While he was lighting it Adrian said again, "The cops came to our house this morning, Shaun! They were looking for you."

"They'll be looking for you if you don't go to school," Shaun replied. "So get moving."

Tod looked at his watch. It was only ten-thirty. He wondered what he was going to do for the rest of the day.

"We can't go to school now," Adrian complained.

"Well, you're not staying up here," Shaun told him. "Go on, get out of here."

Would it be better to go to school now, Tod wondered, and say he'd been held up at home because of the vandals' attack—which was almost true—or go home and tell Grandma he didn't feel well—which almost true too. He really didn't feel very well. He wanted to lie down somewhere in the dark and doze and dream again. Shaun's smell of cigarette smoke and sweat was upsetting him. He wanted to get away from it. Without saying any more to either of the brothers he began to make his way slowly down through the scrub.

"Think about it all," Shaun called after him.

Tod had to make a detour to retrieve his schoolbag. Adrian caught up with him.

"Hey, Tod, let's go into town. I've got some money!"

Tod shook him off. "I'm going home," he said. "I'll see you tomorrow."

"So what are you going to do?" Adrian persisted. "About Shaun and the gang and all that stuff?"

"I don't know," Tod replied.

They parted at the railway crossing. The 10:47 was coming up the track and the bells were going. Tod waited while the train passed and then walked slowly to his grandmother's house. It looked strangely bare and vulnerable without the spiky plants. Grandma had tidied up the slashed leaves and she and Leonie were scrubbing the steps to try and clean them.

"Toddy!" Leonie cried when she saw him. "What are you doing home?"

"Don't feel well," he mumbled.

"Were you upset by last night? I wouldn't be surprised. I feel a bit shaky myself. But why didn't the school phone me? I'd have come and got you."

"Can you phone them, please?" he begged. "And tell them I'm . . ." He stopped, wondering how to phrase it . . . "I'm home today," he finished lamely.

"Of course I will," Leonie cried, taking his arm and leading him inside as if he were a little kid. She put her hand on his forehead. "You haven't got a temperature, have you?"

Tod shook his head. Leonie was overcome by a burst of motherliness and gave him a huge hug. He could smell the cleaner on her hands, together with the background smell of the soap she used and her talcum powder. He leaned against her and breathed it in and for a moment felt quite safe.

"Go and lie down on your bed while I phone the school," Leonie said. "Then I'll bring you a cool drink."

Tod went into his little room. The curtains were still drawn and it was pleasantly dark and cool. He prowled around it, touching his things, the swimming certificate from year five, a ticket from the Power House Museum, a photo of his father on a horse at a trail-riding place.

He went to the bed. Inkspot lay on it, half hidden under the covers. Tod tickled him under his chin. Then he put his face down close to the cat and they touched noses. Inkspot growled softly and Tod growled back at him. He lay down next to the cat and looked around his room. It felt like a little den, like a lair. He closed his eyes and felt his muscles relax. When Leonie came back with a glass of lemonade he was asleep and dreaming.

EIGHT

He was chasing something that twisted and ran in front of him, but he could twist and run just as fast and he was gaining on it. Energy rushed from the earth into him, and the same energy powered the thing that ran from him desperately. They were locked together in an eternal triangle: the predator, the prey, and the earth that sustained them both equally. Nothing had ever been so exciting as this dream hunt, and he could already taste in his mouth the sharp, fierce end to it.

Tod woke up. Inkspot had jumped off the bed and was meowing at the door. The light had changed as the sun moved around the house and it felt like afternoon. Tod lay and looked at the shadows of the leaves on the wall, dappling and shifting. It made everything seem in motion. Nothing stood still. He remembered how, when they first came to Grandma's in the winter, things had seemed so black and white—either good or bad. Now they were all mixed up and he couldn't tell which was which. Perhaps it was part of growing up. He realized with a sudden uncomfortable shock that the term was nearly halfway through. Next term he would be at high school. Unless they made him repeat year seven.

He put that unpleasant thought to the back of his mind

and climbed off the bed. He followed Inkspot out into the garden. Grandma was up the back by the chook run. She waved when she saw Tod.

"Just checking the fence," she called out to him. "Come and give us a hand. And bring the mallet from the shed."

Tod picked it up from the dirt floor of the shed, weighing it in his hand. He liked the way tools felt. He seemed to know by instinct how to hold them and what to do with them. He felt secure with them. He ran up the steps, startling the leghorns who were having a dust bath at the top. They squawked and grumbled at him as he went past, and May tried to peck at his feet.

"The chooks look okay now," he said, handing the mallet to Grandma.

"I'm going to make sure they stay okay too," she muttered. "I'm going to sit out here tonight and wallop that fox devil if he comes back."

"I'll sit up with you," Tod said, excited. "But you haven't got a gun, have you? You aren't going to shoot him?"

"More's the pity," Grandma said. Then spotting the look on Tod's face she grinned at him. "I won't hurt your precious fox, Toddy. I'll just give him a real good scare, so he stays away."

"What about the foxspell?" Tod said. "Won't he put you to sleep?"

"Not if I'm outside, he won't. He only puts the spell on the house. Here, knock those stakes in for me. You've got a good strong arm. I'm going into the house to sleep now. You can wake me up about ten, and we'll sit up together. You can see the fox, and then I'll give him the fright of his life. We'll fix him."

She went slowly down the hill, talking to the hens on the way. They answered her with a contented clucking and went back to scratching little holes in the earth, lowering themselves carefully into them and then throwing the dust over their backs with their wings. The khaki Campbells were lying under the melaleuca bush, their heads under their wings. The first blow of the mallet made the drake open one eye and look at Tod. He closed it again and went back to sleep.

Tod wondered if the ducks dreamed—dreams of water as he dreamed of the earth. Not that they had much water in Grandma's yard—just an old tub that they liked to dip their heads in and throw the water over their backs. They should have a pond. Perhaps he and Grandma could dig one for them.

He knocked in the rest of the stakes and checked the run again. It seemed secure—but then foxes were so clever. Though the fox couldn't get at the chooks tonight because he and Grandma would be sitting up for him. He felt a thrill of excitement. He hadn't spent the night outside since the last of Dad's camping trips. He looked around at the hillside, warm and golden in the westerly sun. The air was clear and still. It was going to be a beautiful, starlit night.

He left the mallet leaning against the side of the run and said good-bye to the poultry. When he went into the house through the back door Dallas was walking in through the front.

"Hi!" she said, sounding rather put out. Leonie was practicing one of her routines and they could hear her voice from the sitting room. Dallas rolled her eyes up at Tod and took her things into the front bedroom she shared with Charm. Two seconds later she was out again.

"Have you seen Charm?" she said quietly to Tod.

"Not since this morning," he replied, not liking to add that it had been at the quarries.

"I'm sure she wasn't at school," Dallas said. "The secretary told me they need a vaccination form back from her so I looked everywhere—not a sign of her."

"She'll be all right," Tod said.

"I'm sure she's all right!" Dallas snapped back. "Charm always is. But she should be at school. She promised Mum she wouldn't ditch here."

"She doesn't like the school."

Dallas made an exasperated noise. "School's got nothing to do with liking it or not. It's what you need to do and you just get on with it."

"Charm's not like that," Tod said. "That works for you, but it doesn't work for her. It's not her fault. It's just the way she's made."

"Sometimes life would be a whole lot easier for everyone if certain people changed the way they're made," Dallas grumbled.

The phone rang. Dallas was next to it so she picked it up. Her voice changed to a pleasant, low tone as she said "Hello." Then she said, "No, it's her sister. Charm's not here, I'm afraid," and put the phone down.

"He's just hung up," she said, looking at Tod. "Do you think he's a boyfriend?"

Tod shrugged. "Could be anyone."

Ten minutes later the phone rang again. This time Tod answered it. He knew it was Shaun who said curtly, "Is Charm there?" and then slammed the phone down, but he didn't tell Dallas. There was no point in worrying her and anyway it was Charm's business.

The phone was to ring three more times before Charm came in. The last time Grandma came stomping out of her room and took the receiver off the hook. "I can't stand all that racket," she snapped. "I'm trying to get a few hours rest. Who the blazes is it that keeps ringing like that?"

"It's someone for Charm," Tod said.

"Can't she call him back?" Leonie said, coming out of the sitting room, dressed in her nighttime gear of slinky black trousers, black-and-silver jacket, silver tie, and long silver earrings. "Where is she, anyway?"

"You look beautiful, Mum," Dallas said, and gave her a hug.

"Thanks, my darling daughter. But don't try and change the subject."

"I wasn't!" Dallas protested. "You really do look gorgeous."

Grandma gave a snort that could have meant anything and retired to her room again. "Don't you forget to wake me," she said to Tod as she closed the door. "If I ever get off to sleep, that is."

Leonie stared after her in bewilderment. "Why's she going to bed now? It's only five o'clock. Is she sick?"

"No, no," Tod reassured her. "She's fine. But we're going to sit up tonight and give the fox a scare. So she's going to get some sleep now and I'm going to wake her up at ten."

"I thought *you* were feeling sick, Tod. You can't stay up all night. What about school tomorrow?"

"I feel fine now," Tod said. "I've been sleeping all day. I'll never get to sleep anyway. I'm not tired at all. Anyway, Grandma already said I could." He looked at his mother with pleading eyes and she must have caught something of his excitement. She grinned back at him and ruffled his hair affectionately. "I suppose it's okay," she said.

"Mum," Dallas protested, "you shouldn't let him. He's got to go to school in the morning."

"It's good for people to stay up all night sometimes," Leonie said. "He'll learn just as much watching out for the fox as he'll learn at school."

"You're so irresponsible." Dallas groaned. "If Charm's started cutting school again it's all your fault."

"Wait a minute," Leonie said. "I thought we were talking about Tod. What's Charm got to do with it?"

"Mum, I don't think she was at school today."

At that moment Charm came in through the back door, her schoolbag over her shoulder. She said nothing to any of her family, just pushed past them and went into the bedroom.

"Charmian," Leonie said sharply. "Come out here. I want to talk to you."

A few moments later Charm came out. "I'm going to have a shower," she mumbled, not looking at her mother.

Leonie seized her arm and tried to get her to turn her face. "Where've you been today?" she demanded.

Dallas and Tod looked at each other and withdrew to the kitchen. They could hear their mother's voice through the wall. Charm didn't seem to be talking at all.

"Here, Tod." Dallas took a potato peeler out of the drawer. "You can help me get something for tea. Peel these potatoes and I'll grill some sausages. We'll have bangers and mash."

It was their father's favorite meal—the one he always cooked for them as a treat. He should have been in the kitchen cooking it for them, but he wasn't, and where he wasn't there was a huge empty space that made him seem impossibly far away. Tod missed him suddenly with an aching physical pain.

"Don't worry," Dallas said, looking at him carefully. "Dad'll come back. It won't be much longer."

"How do you know that?" Tod replied. "How can you be sure he will?"

"I just believe it," Dallas said firmly. "I can't believe he would leave us all forever. I just can't believe it. He would never do that."

She pushed her hair away from her face and smiled at Tod. Then she lit the gas to heat up the grill, and came and helped him.

The potatoes were mashed just the way Tod liked them with lots of butter and salt and the kitchen was full of the smell of sausages when Charm and Leonie came in. Leonie sank into a chair and lit up a cigarette. "This is what you're doing to me," she said dramatically to Charm. "You've driven me to smoking. If I get lung cancer it'll be all your fault."

"You're such a hypocrite," Charm replied. "You're always telling us everyone has to make their own choices. No one's forcing you to smoke." She glared at her mother.

"Just tell me what the problem with school is," Leonie said as if she was repeating something she'd already said several times. "Then I can talk to your teachers and fix things."

"Your problem is you grew up in the sixties," Charm said. "Things can't be fixed anymore, don't you know that?"

"That's nonsense," Leonie cried. "you can always try and do something. It's stupid just to run away from things because you think you can't change them."

Charm shrugged. "You can talk to whoever you like at school. It won't make any difference. It'll probably make things worse."

"Is it because you're missing Laurie?" Leonie said gently.

"Of course I'm missing him!" Charm yelled. "We're all missing him. Isn't that obvious? And I miss Sydney and all my friends. I hate it here! And don't pretend there's something you can do about that because there isn't. Not a single bloody thing!"

"The sausages are ready," Dallas ventured. "Do you want to eat?"

"Stuff the sausages!" Charm cried and ran out of the kitchen. They heard her shout from the passageway. "Who keeps leaving the phone off the hook?" They heard the ping as she replaced the receiver. It began ringing almost immediately.

"Oh, jeez, poor Grandma," Tod said.

"I don't think I can eat anything," Leonie said, lighting another cigarette. "I must get going, I'm supposed to be at the Lion in an hour."

"What am I going to do with all these sausages?" Dallas said.

"We'll eat them tomorrow. Sorry, darling." Leonie gave Tod a kiss as she went by, enveloping him in a mixture of cigarette smoke and perfume. It wasn't a safe smell like the morning one. It was a nighttime smell, exciting and threatening at the same time. "Good hunting," she said from the door. "I hope you see your fox. I'll see you in the morning."

They heard her go out through the back door, and click down the side of the house in her high heels. The engine of the old Citröen coughed as it started up. A few seconds later the brakes squealed in the distance as Leonie took the corner.

Dallas sighed and shook her head. "Have another sausage," she said brightly to Tod.

Despite all the dramas, he was starving. He finished up the mashed potato and ate four more sausages. Tasty as they were, there was something missing, something to do with what he'd been dreaming about before he woke up. He was trying to remember what it was when Charm put the phone down and came back into the kitchen.

"So you didn't go to school either today?" she said to Tod. When she had been talking to her mother before she had seemed closed off, like a sleepwalker. Now she had come alight as if she had been suddenly woken up.

"I wasn't feeling well," he said evasively.

"Ha-ha!" Charm replied, smiling. "You were well enough to be racing around the quarries half the morning."

"What's she talking about?" Dallas demanded. When neither of them answered she went on, "I should do something about you two, I know I should. No one else is going to. But I haven't got time. I've got exams coming up, and I've got a heap of studying to do. So you'll have to sort yourselves out. You can start by cleaning up the kitchen, okay?"

"Thanks for tea, Dallas," Tod called after her.

"Is there anything left?" Charm said, examining the table.

"There's a couple of sausages," Tod said. "I was going to eat them, but you can have them if you want."

Charm made a face. "They look a bit lethal to me. I think I'll throw up if I eat anyway." She clutched her skinny frame dramatically. Her dark eyes were shining with excitement.

"What's up with you?" Tod said, getting up and starting to clear the table.

She shrugged and looked secretive, but she sat down at the table, which, Tod thought, probably meant she wanted to talk about something—or someone.

"That was Shaun on the phone, wasn't it?" he said, as he turned on the tap and squirted the dishwashing liquid into the sink.

"How did you know?"

"He only phoned about ten times this afternoon. That's why we took the phone off the hook. Grandma's trying to sleep and it kept ringing."

Charm made no response to that. Tod said, "What did he say about me?"

"He told me you'd had another little chat." Charm made no effort to move from the table.

"Aren't you going to help?"

"I didn't eat anything," Charm replied, "so I don't have to wash up."

"Aw, come on," he pleaded. "There's way too much for me to do on my own. I didn't tell Mum I saw you at the quarries."

"Did you see me there? I didn't see you. I only knew you were there because Shaun told me." She laughed. "Everyone was up there today!"

"Yeah," Tod muttered, eating the last of the mashed potato out of the saucepan before he dropped it in the soapy water, "regular Central Station."

"So what were you doing up there?" Charm said. "Looking for foxes?"

"Sort of. I just didn't feel like school. I didn't see any, though. Only Adrian and Shaun Stone."

"What did Shaun say to you?"

"Nothing much," Tod replied cautiously. "What did he say to you? You looked angry."

She made a strange face at him, as if warning him to keep out of her life. Tod scrubbed the saucepan for a few seconds and then said, "Why were you angry?"

"He just wanted to move a little too fast. Nothing I can't handle. Anyway, guys like him like angry girls. It turns them on."

"Does he turn you on?"

"Maybe," Charm said. "I like feeling like this."

"Like what?" The whole thing was a mystery to him.

"As if I've got power. Power over him. Power over my life. It's exciting." When he didn't reply she got up and thumped him gently on the shoulder. "You'll understand when you're older," she said. "I'm going to have a shower now."

"What about helping?"

"Leave the things in the drainer," Charm called as she left the kitchen. "I'll put them away later, okay?"

Thinking this was a major concession and that Charm must be in a good mood, Tod went into the sitting room, moved his mother's clothes out of the way, and turned on the TV. He was just settling down to watch it when the phone rang. Charm was still in the shower and probably couldn't hear it, and he didn't want Grandma to be woken again, so he leaped out of the old chair he was sitting in and ran to answer it. He fully expected it to be Shaun, but it was Martin, wondering why he hadn't been at school and if he was sick.

"Adrian wasn't there either," Martin complained. "I had no one to talk to all day."

Tod told him a shortened version of the things that had happened. He mentioned the fox in the yard and the chooks that looked as if they were dead, but he didn't tell him the police had been at their house or that he and Adrian had spent the morning at the quarries. Instead he found himself saying he hadn't been feeling well. He just couldn't be bothered trying to explain everything to Martin.

"I don't know if I'll be at school tomorrow either," he finished. "I'm going to stay up tonight with Grandma to scare the fox away if he comes after the chooks again."

"You are lucky," Martin said wistfully. "My mum would never let me do that. Can you come to my house after school and we'll play computer games?"

Tod said he might, though he knew he wouldn't, and he'd phone anyway. After they'd finished talking he went outside to shut the poultry in the run. They had all put themselves to bed, as they always did at sunset—the ducks in the straw at the back of the shed and the chooks on their perches, May at the top as usual and the little bantams at the bottom. They stirred slightly when they saw him, but they were too sleepy to do more than cluck softly as he pushed the door closed and made sure it was bolted.

The sky over the sea was still flushed with color like ripening apricots, and the evening star was bright. Tod looked toward the quarries where the highest rocks glowed orange. He wondered if the fox was waking up yet and planning its night's hunting. He wasn't tired at all, he couldn't wait for ten o'clock to come so he could wake Grandma. He sat on the top of the steps as it grew slowly darker.

After a while, he began to get restless. To his surprise he realized he was hungry. He'd thought he'd eaten enough sausages to keep him going, but obviously he hadn't. He jumped down the steps and into the dark house, switching the lights on in the kitchen. The light was on in Dallas and Charm's room, and he could hear a radio playing quietly. Dallas must be studying. He wondered if Charm was too, but it didn't seem likely. She had probably gone out with Shaun. He wondered what they were doing and what plans the Breakers had for the night.

Thinking about that made him feel even more restless and hungry. He made himself a cup of hot chocolate and several jam sandwiches and took them into the sitting room, where the TV was still on. Oops, forgot to turn it off, he thought guiltily. He hoped it hadn't disturbed Grandma.

He found a movie to watch, which seemed exciting, even though he'd missed the first half-hour and couldn't follow the plot. Every few minutes he glanced toward the clock and the hands slowly inched their way round to ten. At last it was time to wake Grandma.

He knocked on the door and when there was no answer,

opened it and put on the light. Grandma sat straight up in bed. She blinked at Tod a couple of times and then smiled at him. "Ten, is it?" she said briskly. She swung her legs off the bed and stood up. "Put the kettle on, there's a good lad," she said. "If we're sitting up all night we'll need something hot."

Grandma filled a thermos with hot tea and put it in a box with two cups, a cask of port, a packet of cookies, and a bar of chocolate. She took the big flashlight from the laundry shelf and two old sleeping bags from the top of one of the wardrobes.

"Don't think I've used these since your grandfather died," she muttered, holding them up to her nose and smelling them. "Gor, they pong a bit, but they'll keep us warm."

"Did you and Grandpa go camping?" Tod said as they bundled up the sleeping bags and stacked them on top of the box.

"Ken loved the bush," Grandma said. "We used to go up to the Flinders Ranges and down the Southeast too, down the Coorong." She picked up the box with the bags and held them out to Tod. "Here, you carry these, and I'll bring the flashlight."

Outside on the back veranda she collected a couple of old cushions from the cane chaise lounge.

"Why don't you go anymore?" Tod asked as they clambered up the steps.

"Wassat?"

"Why don't you go camping now?"

Grandma was shining the flashlight down on the ground so Tod could see where to put his feet. "I never really fancied it on my own," she said quietly. "I'd love to go back to some of that country, but it wouldn't be the same without Ken. Do you remember him at all, Toddy?"

Tod tried to remember, but he wasn't sure if he was remembering or seeing the photos of his grandfather in his mind. "Not really," he said. "I wish I did."

Grandma took the sleeping bags from the top of the box and dropped them on the ground under the melaleuca. Then she helped Tod with the box.

"You would only have been four or five when he died," she said as they crawled into the bags and settled themselves down with a cushion each. Grandma propped herself up against the trunk of the melaleuca and Tod lay flat on his back looking up through the feathery branches at the night sky. "But I wish you'd known him. You'd have got on like a house on fire, the pair of you. He was just like you, mad about animals and the bush and all that."

"I'll come camping with you," Tod suggested. "Dad could take us when he comes back. We used to go with him in New South Wales."

"If he comes back, we'll do that," Grandma promised.

Tod didn't care for the *if* and the tone of her voice as she spoke. He thought about it for a few moments and then said, "You know, the ducks need water. We should dig them a pond."

"You're right, they do," Grandma agreed cheerfully. "We should dig it now before the ground gets too hard. You can start it tomorrow—if you're not too tired, that is."

"I'm not tired at all now," Tod said. Even though he was lying down he felt extremely alert, as though he could leap to his feet at any moment and run tirelessly through the night and chase and hunt. . . .

"I'm hungry though!" he said.

"Already?" Grandma teased him. "You'll have to go back to base camp again and stock up with provisions." She passed him the packet of cookies. He tore it open and ate four. They were chocolate and wheatmeal and he could have eaten the whole pack, but then he remembered he should share them, so he offered them to Grandma. She was pouring port into her cup. "Not for the moment, thanks, Toddy. Save them for later. Here, have a sip of this. It'll keep you warm."

The port smelled fruity with a hint of rotten grapes to it. Tod took a sip and screwed up his nose. He didn't like the taste, but when the port hit his stomach he could feel the warmth spreading through him. He took another sip.

"Steady on," Grandma said. "Leave some for me."

Tod handed the cup back to her and lay down again. "What are you going to scare the fox with?" he asked.

"That's a thought," Grandma said. "I'll need something to chuck at the old devil. Take the flashlight and see if you can find some stones."

Tod wriggled out of the sleeping bag again and switched on the flashlight. The beam was as strong as a searchlight. He flashed it up into the trees and spotted two white birds roosting above them. Cockatoos, probably. Then he shone it into the poultry run. The chooks complained softly. The light picked out the mallet which he had left leaning against the fence. Tod picked it up and handed it to Grandma.

"Here, Grandma, you can whack him with this!"

He went to the back fence where there was a pile of rocks Grandma had cleared out of the garden. They'd used some of them when they'd been rebuilding the run. Tod carried back a few of the smaller ones and piled them under the melaleuca within easy reach. When he settled down again and switched off the light the night seemed much darker and the stars brighter. Grandma passed him a cup of tea and a piece of chocolate.

"There's Orion's belt," he said. It was one of the constellations his father had pointed out as being in both the northern and southern skies. "Dad used to say he was upside down." He remembered too how much his father had missed the northern stars, especially the Great Bear. But to make up for that you had the beautiful Southern Cross. He wriggled around trying to see it.

"Can you see the Southern Cross, Grandma?"

"We can't see it yet. It's too low in the sky—it'll be behind the hill. It'll come up later. The Nungas call it the Eagle's foot, you know. Ken used to know all the old stories about the stars and the land. He'd tell them to me and the girls while we were lying out at night just like this."

"Tell me some now," Tod said. "Are there any stories about this place?"

"I don't know any about this particular bit of hillside. I wish I did. It must have had a whole heap of stories attached to it, and now the land's been altered out of all recognizing, and the stories gone forever." Grandma sighed. "But I know a few that are set in and around Adelaide—or Tandanya we should really call it—the place of the red kangaroo dreaming."

She told him the story of Ngurunderi and his Dreamtime journey down the Murray in pursuit of his two wives, and of Tjilbruke, the ibis man, whose nephew was killed close by on the Sturt River at Marion, and the story of Pootpobberie, half man and half kangaroo.

"Can people be turned into animals?" Tod said dreamily. Two owls were calling to each other in the distance: *boobook boobook.*

"If you believe the old stories they can. Now we'd better shut up if we want to see that old fox. If he hears voices he'll be miles away."

Tod heard the last passenger train for the night go by, and a little after that a freight train. He heard his mother come home in the Citroën. The sounds of the city faded as the traffic thinned. The wind got up and he could hear the trees creaking as though they were trying to talk. He turned carefully over in his sleeping bag, and lay like an animal resting its head on its paws. He fell into the light dozing dreaming state he had been in on the hillside that morning. He could hear everything, yet he was dreaming.

The night went by. The stars wheeled overhead. The earth turned toward the sun.

Tod could feel the fox coming toward him. Sometimes it looked like a fox and sometimes like a man, as if like Pootpobberie it was half man and half animal.

Everything—the humans in their houses and the poultry in their pens—was in a deep sleep, but the fox sleep couldn't touch him because he was a fox himself. This sudden realization made him open his eyes, and the fox was standing by the henhouse two yards away from him.

Tod put out his hand and touched Grandma. She was awake, the mallet in her hand. She hurled it with astonishing strength at the fox. The animal gave an almost human cry of surprise and pain, and then it fled like a shadow toward the back fence.

Tod's first instinct was to run, but he was trapped inside the sleeping bag and he fell over and almost rolled down the hill. By the time he had struggled out of the bag and found his feet, the fox had disappeared.

Grandma had jumped out of her bag and was retrieving the mallet. The chooks gave a squawk of complaint about being woken up so early.

"You hit him!" Tod said in awe to Grandma.

"Good shot, eh?" she cackled, and waved the mallet in the air. "I always was a deadeye. If I'd have had me gun, the blighter would be dead. I've given him something to think about anyway. He won't be back in a hurry."

Tod had never seen her so excited. She was dancing around the yard, still waving the mallet, and calling out to the chooks. "You're safe this time, me darlings. We saved you. Bop! We got the fox!"

The chooks squawked even louder.

He wasn't sure whether to be sorry or pleased. He hadn't wanted the fox to be hurt. But it had been really exciting to wait for it and see it come, and, he had to confess it to himself, to see Grandma hit it. It reminded him of the hunting feeling from his dreams. He shivered.

Grandma stopped her dancing and looked at him. "You're cold," she said. "Come on, we'll go in now. He won't be back tonight. Time for a couple of hours sleep before morning." She poured herself a drop of port and took a swig. Tod shuddered. The idea of the alcohol on an empty predawn stomach made him feel sick.

There was a long, low hooting from down the hill and the ground began to shake. The early morning freight train was on its way through to Melbourne. The bells began to ring at the level crossing, like an alarm clock to wake everyone up, Tod thought, as he stumbled down the steps and into the house. Grandma put the lights on, and they looked unnaturally harsh and bright. The house inside looked strange as if everything had grown old and dirty while they were outside in the fresh night air. Or perhaps it was just that he was suddenly aching with tiredness. Grandma dumped the sleeping bags on the laundry floor, saying she would wash them later, and poured herself a cup of tea from the thermos. She took it into the bedroom with her and Tod fell into his own bed. He slept immediately.

NINE

When Tod woke up it was bright daylight. A train was clattering down the hill toward the city. Perhaps it was the 12:01 or the 1:01. Tod yawned and stretched, not bothering to check his watch. There was no need to get up yet, he thought lazily. No need to move until the sun disappeared from the sky and night fell. But he didn't exactly think it in words, and he didn't think about precise times either. He saw a series of images inside his head—the sun, the night, himself set within each frame, part of the sun, part of the night, not a person who thought things out and planned them with clocks and dates and timetables.

He yawned again. He was changing inside in some way, but he wasn't sure what he was changing into.

Then the door opened and his mother came into the room. The images disappeared and he was back to his old way of thinking again. He didn't feel like getting up. He wanted to stay in bed and work out what was happening to him, so he lay with his eyes closed and hoped she would go away again. But Leonie was in a brisk and bossy mood. She shook Tod awake and made him get up.

She made him lunch and told him he could go to school for the afternoon, and since she was going out she would drop him there on the way. Tod wasn't sure how much Dallas had said to her, but Leonie must have been a bit suspicious, because she sat in the car for a few minutes and watched him to make sure he went in.

Ms. Linkman was trying to interest the class in English grammar, but Tod's thoughts kept wandering. They wandered over the quarries, searched for the big fox, thought about Grandma's stories and about people who could be half animal and half man, and ended up outside the strange camp in the cave, staring at the fire.

Tod couldn't understand why he hadn't been able to find the way through the ash trees when he had been there with Adrian. He kept thinking about all the different paths and tracks he had explored, running through them in his mind with his new way of thinking as if he were watching himself running along them, ears pointed, tail swinging.

Martin nudged him. "Stop making that funny noise," he muttered.

"What noise?"

"Like you're panting."

"I'm not making any noise," Tod said.

"Yes, you are," Adrian put in.

Ms. Linkman stopped in midstream. "Are you listening, Adrian?"

"Yes," he assured her innocently.

"So what was I saying?"

"It's wrong to put the apostrophe in *its* when it means *of it,*" Martin said swiftly.

"I wasn't asking you, Martin, I'm sure you know this already. Tod and Adrian, do you understand it?"

They both nodded their heads. Ms. Linkman sighed and went on.

Finally the lesson was over and they packed up their books before the siren went.

"Are you coming to my house?" Martin asked Tod.

Tod had forgotten he'd said he might go and play computer games again. He had been thinking about going to the quarries all afternoon. He couldn't bear not to go now.

"I could come a bit later," he replied, not wanting to hurt Martin's feelings. "I just want to check something out first."

"I'll come to your house, Marty," Adrian said promptly. "Can we play that brilliant new game of yours?"

Martin looked very uncomfortable. "Perhaps we'd better make it another time."

Adrian put on his proud face. "I forgot, I've got to rehearse something anyway. I can't come today." He walked away from them both, his back stiff with outrage.

"What was that about?" Tod said curiously.

Martin looked even more embarrassed. "My mum doesn't like him coming to our house. She thinks he's a bad influence. Because of his brother mainly."

Tod didn't know what to say. Martin added after a few minutes, "She thinks you're all right. She doesn't want me to hang around the quarries with you but you can come to our house."

Tod didn't like to say he thought Martin's life was incredibly boring. "Well, I might come around later," he said vaguely.

"Do you think you could phone if you're not coming? Otherwise she'll worry that you've got lost." Martin saw Tod's expression and added defensively, "She just worries a lot about everything."

"Well, you'd better hurry along home, else she'll be worrying about you," Tod retorted. Martin and his mother were starting to irritate him. And he wanted to get moving. He felt as if he wanted to run and run. He couldn't stop himself breaking into a trot. "See you later," he shouted to Martin and ran all the way home.

He arrived there at the same time as the postman on his noisy yellow motorbike. "There you go, mate," the man said, handing the letters to Tod. Tod's heart jumped when he saw the blue and red stripes of the aerogram. He ran inside shouting, "There's a letter from Dad!"

The house seemed empty, but as he went into the laundry Grandma's door opened and she came rather sleepily out into the passageway. "Hello, Toddy," she said, yawning. "You're up then. Give us the post."

"I've been to school and everything," he said. "Look, Dad's written us another letter."

Grandma didn't say anything, just made her usual snorting noise as she went into the kitchen to put the kettle on.

Tod dropped his schoolbag on the laundry floor and carefully opened the letter. Laurie's writing was really difficult to read. He wondered if he should leave it till Leonie or Dallas got home and they could read it to him. But the letter was a tangible part of his father and he couldn't bear to put it down. He put it up to his nose and smelled it; there was no trace of Laurie's smell left on it, just the chilly odor of airplanes and a slight smell of ink. He went into his room to change into his old jeans and then he folded the letter up and put it in his back pocket.

He went into the kitchen to get something to eat. Grandma was sitting at the kitchen table drinking a cup of tea.

"That was fun last night," Tod said, taking out a slice of bread and spreading it with butter and jam.

"I'm getting too old for that sort of thing," Grandma said, shaking her head. "I'm knackered today."

"Do you think you hurt the fox?"

"I reckon we gave him a good fright," Grandma said, smiling slightly. "You off to the quarries again?"

Tod nodded, his mouth full of bread.

"Well, don't be back late or Dallas'll be after my hide for not stopping you." Grandma poured herself another cup of tea and lit a cigarette.

"And tell that old devil to stay away from my chooks!" she shouted after Tod as he left the house.

After the mild night it had been a beautiful day but when Tod went outside again he realized the weather was changing. A brisk wind was getting up, cold and damp on his face and ears. He put his head up and sniffed the air. He could smell rain coming. Away to the southwest a bank of cloud was approaching like a huge wave. He began to run.

At the railway he had to wait for the express to pass. Tired pale faces observed him indifferently through the windows. No one waved. When the train had gone he jumped across the tracks and trotted swiftly up the lane.

At the top of the path that led down to the gully he stopped and sniffed again. He could smell humans, a particular smell of sweat and cigarette smoke that he recognized and that made the hair stand up on the back of his neck. He trod very lightly going down the path and across the creek. At the waterhole he knelt and lapped.

The wind was getting stronger and a few drops of rain hit him on the neck, but the magpies were warbling gently in the gums up the slope and he knew this meant there was nothing dangerous about. He padded up the hill, dropping onto all fours when the going got steeper, listening all the time to the web of noise around him, picking out anything that might spell danger.

The rain fell more heavily, bringing a strong smell of dust and earth. A magpie shrieked and he heard the anxious flap of its wings. He froze where he was, flattening himself into the ground. A few seconds later he heard voices ahead, coming from the high grassy area where he and Adrian had seen the snakeskin. The smell of cigarette smoke became much stronger.

Thinking without words again, hardly realizing he was doing it, Tod saw in his mind three figures lounging at the top of the hill. One was Shaun, another was the dark greyhound boy, Dom, and the third was the one called Justin, with the thick white neck. He saw the gun in Shaun's hand. He heard his voice, *you can be the fox . . . we'll hunt you. . . .*

Common sense should have told him to creep silently away, but he wasn't thinking with human common sense anymore. He wanted to get to the big quarry. Something was drawing him there. He wanted to find the camp again, examine the strange implements, see if the fire was lit. . . .

So he padded on. The track he was following led straight up into the area now blocked by the Breakers. But if he cut off to his right through the scrub he would hit upon another higher track, a very narrow one used only by animals, which would lead him across the top of the slope to where the big quarry was—or rather where it had been the previous times he'd run up there, for now he recalled what had happened the day before and the weird sense of disorientation he'd had when he couldn't find the tunnel that led through the rocks. The road had been in the way, he remembered. Listening now for the noise of traffic, he could hear in the distance the harsh grunting of trucks as they changed gear for the hill and the squeal of brakes as someone took the corner too fast.

Picking out from the whole web of sounds the ones that concerned him, he continued through the scrub, trying to move quietly, noticing how much harder it was off the track. Every leaf and twig under his feet seemed to crackle or rustle.

He was nearly at the top, within hand's reach of the smaller track he was heading for, when he heard the voices grow louder. He looked back over his shoulder and saw the three boys on the track below. He made a leap for the shelter of the olive bushes above him, but the steep slope was slippery with wet leaves and he lost his footing. It was only a stumble, but the noise attracted the attention of the gang. The voices were instantly silent. As Tod grabbed at an olive branch and pulled himself up and onto the track he heard a tiny click that terrified him. He threw himself forward, scrambling at top speed. There was another, louder crack behind him. He could hear crashing in the bushes below. They were after him. They were going to get him. They were going to kill him.

A kaleidoscope of images, sounds, and smells whirled in his brain. He saw a fox fall to the earth, its spirit returning to the place it came from. He felt again his dream of the hunt, and realized he was both the hunter and the prey. And right in front of him he saw a huge fox. It was so close it was touching noses with him. He smelled its strong smell as it breathed on him.

Images formed in his mind. He saw the darkness of the dream quarry. He saw a safe place, the glow of firelight. He saw himself following the big fox, and immediately that was what he was doing.

Tod bounded on all fours up the slope. The big fox had disappeared, but he could follow its scent. The rain made it clear and rank. He could hear the boys behind him; he thought he heard Shaun shout something, and his skin prickled with the thought that at any moment they might take another shot at him and this time they might hit him.

The rain swept over in great squally waves. Tod was soaked to the skin, water dripping off his hair and nose. He realized with relief that the slope was lessening. He was nearly at the top. His heart was aching in his chest and his legs were shaking as he ran, on his two feet now, into the shelter of the ash trees, into the familiar darkness. The voices behind him were cut off abruptly. He plodded on through the darkness and the silence.

Following the scent of the fox, he had no trouble finding the tunnel through the fallen rocks. When he had crawled through it and struggled to his feet on the other side, the first thing he saw was firelight, bright in the dusk.

Next to the fire sat a man. At first Tod thought he was young but his skin looked worn as if he were old, and when he jumped to his feet to come closer he limped.

"You here," he said. *"Yarp,* at last we meet *here ere ere!"*

Tod said nothing, just stared at him. The man was wearing clothes so old they seemed to merge with his skin. His feet were bare, brown, and leathery, and his reddish, wavy hair was held back from his forehead by a leather headband. His hair was rather long and his ears pointy. His eyes were green and bright, and his mouth had a twist in it as though he were about to start laughing.

"You scared?" he went on, when Tod didn't speak. "Not scare of *me ee ee?* Not hurt you. I like you *yarp yarp!"* His whole face crinkled up as he grinned. "Come," he went on more gently. "Come to *fire ire ire."*

With one last stab at reality Tod said, "I must go home."

The man grinned more widely, showing his sharp white teeth. *"Hooome,"* he howled. "You *hooome* here. You *hooome* now with *me ee ee."*

He led Tod toward the fire, and squatted down by it. In the firelight his face and hair shone reddish brown. He looked up at Tod with eyes so bright and knowing, Tod could not hold his gaze.

"You know who I am *yarp*?"

Tod shook his head.

"Yarp, you know," the other said. He stood again and put out his hand. Taking Tod under the chin he turned his head so he could look him directly in the eyes.

Tod knew those eyes, he knew the wild feeling that leaped from them, but he couldn't believe what he knew.

"Old woman good *snarrul* shot." The man tapped himself on the leg. "That hurt."

"You're the fox?" Tod said slowly.

"Yarp!" The man smiled, showing again his neat white teeth. "I fox-man. Fox spirit. One time humans named me Dan Russell *snarrul.* Dan Russell my *na ame ame."*

Tod stared at him in amazement. He went on, "You called. You *ca all alled* like a hurt cub. I heard you speak to my dead child. *Snarrul.* You put its body back in earth. So when you called, I *ca ame ame."*

"Where did you come from?"

"From here. *Yarp!* You called me out from *he ere ere."* He waved around the darkening quarry and made a scooping gesture as though he was digging something up out of the earth.

"You mean, you're here all the time? How come no one knows about you?"

Dan Russell drew his gingery eyebrows together in a frown. "This secret place. Spirit place. *Snarrul.* No human comes here unless spirit being leads them."

"I tried to get here yesterday," Tod said. "The road was in the way."

"Road!" Dan Russell spat with disgust. "*Snarrul.* Road does not bother spirit people. We here long before *ro oa oad.*" He smiled again with a sudden change of expression. "Eat!" he announced.

Tod's chest and legs were no longer aching and the fire was warming him. He stretched out on the dry earth under the shelter of the rock ledge. He was ravenously hungry. Dan Russell cut a piece of meat from something that looked like a dead rabbit and handed it to him. Part of Tod thought it smelled disgusting and the other part of him started salivating.

"Don't you cook it?" he said.

Dan Russell grinned at him from the other side of the fire. "Raw, cooked, all the same to *me ee ee,*" he barked. *"Yarp! Yarp!"*

Tod sank his teeth into it and tore the flesh from the bone. It was springy and chewy, and it tasted better than anything he'd ever had in his life. He took another piece and then drank from the iron pot of water. The water tasted amazing too, clean and sweet and completely thirst quenching.

Dan Russell watched him all the time with his bright green eyes.

"You like foxes *yarp*?" he said when Tod had finished.

"I was interested," Tod said. "I wanted to know about them. I thought you were just an ordinary fox." He wiped his hands on the rock next to him. "I'm sorry Grandma hit you," he added. "She wanted to scare you away from her chooks."

Dan Russell smacked his lips together. "Humans hate me and my children. *Snarrul.* They kill my children. What do humans do all day, but dream up new ways to kill my children? I've seen all—hunt with dogs, shoot with guns, poison food, poison *air air air.* But you gave my dead child back to the earth. *Yarp.* I do something for you. *Yarp.* Spirit world pays back. . . ." He grinned again at Tod without explaining further.

"You've already done one thing," Tod said. "I reckon you might have saved me from the gang—those boys who were after me. They were hunting me, they were trying to kill me!"

"Those humans kill my children," Dan Russell said, somber. "One day *snarrul* they will pay. But you did good thing for my child, *yarp,* I do good thing for *you ou ou.*" His eyes gleamed in the firelight. "Watch."

His skin began to ripple and swirl. His clothes dissolved into red-brown fur. His eyes gleamed brighter and brighter as his face changed to a fox's mask, and his ears pointed and turned forward. His feet and hands shrank to neat paws and his nails turned into black claws. He smiled at Tod and showed a red tongue and sharp white teeth.

Tod was enthralled. The fox sat before him, so close he could touch it. He felt its fur, remembering the fox that had been dead. This fox was alive, more than alive. It was the distilled essence of every fox that had ever lived. It was pure fox.

Then the process happened in reverse and the fox-man stood before him again.

"I do this for *you ou ou,*" he barked. "*Yarp,* I let you be fox."

As soon as it happened Tod realized it had been going to happen all along. Everything had been leading to this point. Dan Russell turned back into his fox form and stared deep into Tod's eyes. The wild feeling leaped again, leaped right through with nothing blocking it. It flowed through Tod, fifty times stronger than Grandma's port, and he felt his body turn and change, but not strangely. His new body was familiar to him from his dreams, and he felt as much at home in it as in his old one. He ran his pointy red tongue around his sharp teeth and swished his white-tipped brush, licked his neat paws a couple of times and grinned at the big fox standing next to him.

Dan Russell grinned back. He looked very pleased with himself.

Tod opened his mouth to say something, but no words came out. He barked in surprise. The noise made him lose his balance, and he sat down suddenly on his haunches. He wasn't used to sitting with four legs and it took him a while to get the hang of it. He kept falling over.

Dan Russell was laughing at him. Tod knew he was telling him he was just a cub and had a lot to learn, but he couldn't work out how he knew it. He seemed to receive images from Dan Russell, both from external signals like the way his ears moved or the way he held his head, and from some collective pool shared by the foxes. Instant pictures leaped into Tod's mind in response to the world around him. His senses were sharp and alert to everything. They were far more acute than when he had been a human.

Once the foxes moved out from the shelter of the cave he was overwhelmed by a mass of smells and sounds. He spent a long time sitting next to Dan Russell trying to sort out what he was hearing and smelling. Then he had to practice moving like a shadow through the undergrowth on the quarry floor, learning how to feel the earth beneath each paw, using its energy as though he were growing out of it. He had to use the same energy to give him spring when he leaped from boulder to boulder like a cat. Every time he made a mistake Dan Russell snarled at him, showing sharp white teeth, and then shook with silent laughter when Tod did something particularly clumsy, like missing the boulder he was aiming for and sliding down into a prickly kangaroo thorn.

He was panting, his legs were aching, and his nose and paws were sore but Dan Russell wouldn't let him stop.

Tod saw deep in his mind the perseverance and the stamina of the fox. He saw pictures that awed and frightened him of foxes outrunning hounds, pushing beyond exhaustion to get away. He saw the cunning of the pursued animal, and the strength that terror gave. He learned the fox could never give up, because it had to outlast the enemy who was always after it, and he saw what happened to the fox that didn't outlast the enemy. It made him shudder.

And when Tod thought he would die from tiredness and pain he found something deep inside his fox self that enabled him to go on.

Finally they returned to the cave. The rain had eased but it was still drizzly and damp. Tod noticed with pleasure how the water ran off his dense fox coat without penetrating through to the skin. He was much drier and warmer than he would be if he'd been wearing clothes in the rain. He went to the iron pot and lapped from the water. Then he sniffed around the cave looking for food. He found a rabbit bone and carried it to the entrance. When Dan Russell came closer he growled softly at him.

He felt the big fox's approval and knew he had learned fast. He looked at him and saw the thick red coat start to ripple and dissolve. He saw the flow and glimmer of limbs and then Dan Russell stood before him as a man. He smiled at Tod and bent to rekindle the fire. The smell of the smoke reminded Tod of all sorts of things—human things. He saw a clear picture of a family in a house down near the railway. They looked sad.

Someone was missing. With a deep sigh he finished crunching up the bone.

Dan Russell was watching him carefully with his green eyes, and Tod thought he could now read something other than approval in them. Dan Russell didn't want him to think about home or about his human life. Perhaps Dan Russell wanted him to stay a fox forever. The thought made him whimper slightly. The home picture became stronger and clearer. He sent the message to Dan Russell as urgently as he could.

The piercing eyes held his and the wild feeling drained out of him. With a mixture of relief and regret he felt himself begin to change.

When he was human again he thought of all sorts of things he wanted to ask. He knew he had to get home, but he simply had to find out a bit more first. He squatted down on the ground next to Dan Russell and stared into the flames.

"Why do you have a fire?" he said. "If you're a spirit being? And do you live forever? And where do you come from? And if you're the fox spirit why do you sometimes look like a person?"

Dan Russell yapped with laughter again. "All spirit beings can look like people *yarp yarp*! Sometimes we people, sometimes animals, plants, rocks, birds. Humans use speech and *fi ire ire.* Spirit people like to use *too oo oo.*"

Beyond the firelight the quarry was dark and mysterious. Dan Russell gestured to it.

"This spirit place *yarp.* Alongside human time runs spirit time. Here everything goes on *forever ever ever.* Spirit fox lives forever. In your time, fox die *snarrul* all things die and return to *ur ur earth.*"

"How did you get here?" Tod said, trying to puzzle it all out. "You can't always have been here." He thought about the original inhabitants of the land and the stories Grandma had told him about Ngurunderi and Tjilbruke. "Foxes haven't always been here. Did you come when the first foxes came?"

Dan Russell wasn't grinning anymore. His thin face was somber and his green eyes had gone dark. "Humans took my children away from own land," he snarled. "Who can understand why? Humans have gone *snarrul* so far from spirit world no one can understand them. *Yarp*, they hate my children, but in new land *snarrul* they miss them. They have nothing to hunt. So they bring my children here, in cages on ships."

The thought of it made the fox-man howl in rage.

Tod could imagine the terrified foxes trapped in cramped, dirty cages on the old ships that took months to get from England to Australia.

"This strange land with strange stars and strange earth *snarrul*," Dan Russell went on. "My children call out to me from this strange land. *We have no lan an and. We are lo o ost. Our feet bur ur urn. We cannot touch the ur ur earth.* So I come *yarp yarp*. Teach them to live here in this new land, look after them."

"How did you get here? And what about your children back where you came from?"

"Spirit place, spirit *ti i ime*," Dan Russell said mysteriously. "We have own way of being, own laws, *yarp*. Part of us lives forever in the deep bones of earth, in the hollow hills. There are ways into earth *snarrul*, entrances to spirit world. In the beginning all creatures lived in own place with own spirit beings *yarp*. But humans grew restless *snarrul*. They wanted to wander over whole earth. They took animals and plants with them. Spirit beings must follow their children *yarp*. Humans cut open *ur ur earth*, and let out the part that dwells in its *bo o ones*. Humans cut earth *snarrul*—" he made a fierce slashing gesture round at the quarry—"and we slip through. They let us through to new place *yarp yarp*."

The thought of it seemed to please him. His face lightened and he grinned at Tod. "All human things affect spirit world," he told him. "And all spirit things human world. No creature escapes that *snarrul*."

Tod wasn't sure he understood what the fox-man was saying but he liked the sound of it. It was fascinating to think of all the new plants and animals that had been introduced into Australia, each with its spirit. "Who else came from the other side of the world?" he asked.

"All things have their own guardians, *yarp*," Dan Russell replied. "Look at trees. Ash and Olive guardians live *he e ere*."

Tod looked toward the end of the quarry where the rocks and boulders formed a wall. He could just make out two shapes among the shadows of the trees. A man and woman stood side by side. They were enormously tall and their heads were turned toward each other as if they were talking.

"Yggdrasil and *snarrul* Athene," Dan Russell said offhandedly. "Always talking, *yarp*. They weak now. Trees move *slow ow ow*. Wait till stronger. They work on changing land for own children. They take over creeks. They make more *rai ai ain*." He shook his head and howled quietly. "Humans don't know what they let out *snarrul* when they cut *ur ur earth*!"

"What about the guardians of the things that were here already?" Tod said, remembering how Ms. Livetti seemed to prefer native animals to foxes. "Don't the gum trees have a guardian? And the native animals? Didn't their guardians try and stop you moving in?"

Dan Russell's green eyes narrowed and his face twisted. "I only look after own children *snarrul*," he snapped. Tod thought he was going to say something else, but he was silent.

"I'd better go home," Tod said after a few moments.

"I didn't know, *yarp*," Dan Russell said abruptly. "I didn't know they weren't the same as rabbits *snarrul*."

"What?"

"When my children first came, plenty food animals *yarp yarp*. Little hopping animals like rabbits *snarrul*. Their guardians weak. Couldn't make enough of them to feed us. Guardian spirits faded and little animals disappeared *snarrul*."

"Your children ate them all," Tod said. "I bet you're sorry."

"Sorry?" Dan Russell said. "What does sorry mean? You mean hungry *yarp*?"

"No, not hungry. Like sad that all the little animals disappeared."

"Sad for my children that they eat human rubbish *now ow ow*," Dan Russell howled.

"At least your children aren't extinct."

"You only *snarrul* human," Dan Russell replied scathingly. "You know nothing *snarrul*."

Tod looked at the strange world around him. Beyond the firelight he thought he could see other shapes moving. He realized he knew absolutely nothing about anything. He wanted to learn, but he was beginning to feel frightened. Dan Russell didn't think like a person at all. Tod remembered that when he had been a fox everything Dan Russell had communicated had been true, and he'd obeyed him immediately. It was only being human again that made him doubtful and scared. His fox mind had been clear and straightforward, and linked directly to his body. A fox wouldn't have stood here now, scuffling its feet and wondering what to do. He wanted more than anything else to feel that certainty again.

"Then will you teach me?" he said.

"*Yarp yarp,*" Dan Russell snapped. "For my dead child's sake."

"Can I come back then?" Tod said. When Dan Russell did not respond he pleaded, "If I come back will you let me in?"

"Watch at full *moo oo oon,*" Dan Russell said. "I come where you live. Don't let old woman know *snarrul.*"

Tod nodded and turned to go. He looked back once to wave, but Dan Russell was staring into the flames and did not see him.

Beyond the glow of the fire it was dark and shadowy. The two tree spirits were having an earnest discussion. He could hear their soft voices like the rustling of leaves. They fell silent as he approached and bent their lofty heads down to watch him pass, but they said nothing to him, and he said nothing either, since he had absolutely no idea what to say to a tree spirit.

When he had wriggled through the tunnel and come out into the everyday world, he had no idea about anything else either. His mind was completely blank. The only thing that kept him going was the thought of home. He was aching all over and it was almost pitch dark, but his fox senses were working. His eyes adapted quickly to the night, and he followed the smell of his own track back down the hill and through the tangled bushes.

The faint smell of the Breakers lingered on the damp earth, but much stronger was the distinctive scent of the olive and ash trees. Tod could feel them stretching in the rain, which was falling more heavily again. They loved it, especially the ashes. It made them grow more thickly, made them spread. He thought he could sense the gum trees retreating. He shook himself and shivered. His clothes were soaked. He missed his fox coat.

TEN

Someone was at the end of the lane. Tod could see the figure leaning against the railing, dark against the bright lights
at the gate to the depot. He hesitated for a moment, then
decided he wasn't going to let anyone stop him taking the
quickest way home. He was too cold and tired, and anyway his
mind was full of fox thoughts.

"So how did you like being the fox?" Tod had smelled
Shaun long before he spoke. Shaun's voice, his stance, everything about him spelled out *no danger.* He was on his own and
wasn't carrying the gun. Tod had been going to trot past without speaking, but Shaun's question made him stop. How could
Shaun know what had happened? He stared at him for a few
moments, hardly breathing.

"Justin tried to shoot you," Shaun went on. Tod breathed
out sharply. Of course, Shaun was talking about the threat
he'd made about hunting Tod, that was all.

"It wasn't me, truly. Lucky it wasn't. I might not have
missed."

"You shouldn't shoot the foxes," Tod burst out. "What have
they done to you? Just leave them alone!"

"We've got to shoot something," Shaun said. "And foxes
are pests. That's why it was no fun really hunting you,

because I knew I wasn't going to try and shoot you at the end."

Tod didn't reply.

"You used to be able to get money for fox skins. That's what Justin's dad told him. But no one wants them anymore."

The foxes want them, Tod thought, shivering again. He turned to cross the road. Shaun followed him.

"So where did you disappear to? We searched the place for you. You must be good at hiding yourself."

Tod couldn't help smiling to himself. Shaun came alongside him and they walked in an almost companionable fashion over the railway line and down Tod's street.

"Your sister home?"

"How do I know?"

"Here." Shaun brought something out of his pocket and gave it to Tod. It was too dark to see what it was, but it felt like a chocolate bar. "I'm glad Justin missed you."

"You'd have been in real trouble if he'd hit me," Tod said. He was hungry again and his mouth was watering at the thought of the chocolate. He stopped under the streetlamp and unwrapped the bar. "Thanks," he mumbled to Shaun as he crammed it in his mouth.

"Tell Charm I'm out here," Shaun said.

Tod left him in the reserve. At the front gate he turned to look back at him. Shaun gave him a wave. There was something attractive about the gesture, Tod thought, as though Shaun were treating him as an equal. He laughed to himself, a little snappy fox laugh.

Dallas shouted from the kitchen when he came through the back door. "Is that you, Tod? Where on earth have you been? I've been worried sick."

"It's okay," he shouted back loudly. "I'm fine."

She came bustling out of the kitchen. "Oh, look at you! You're soaking wet!"

"Stop fussing so much," he said. She was making him angry with her mothering. She still treated him as if he were six. Didn't she realize he was growing up?

"Get those wet things off, and put them in the laundry," she said. "I'll wash them in the morning. Do you know what time it is?"

"I suppose you're about to tell me!"

"Yes, I am! It's nearly nine o'clock. You shouldn't be wandering around outside at this time of night. Tell me where you've been."

"I was up at the quarries, Dallas, if it's any of your business!"

"Don't talk to me like that! I'm only trying to look after you! No one else does. Mum's gone racing off again, leaving me to do all the worrying!"

"Don't worry then," Tod snapped. "No one's making you." He went angrily down to his room and pushed the chair against the door so Dallas couldn't break in on him. He was terrified she was going to come and undress him herself. As he came out in dry clothes, dropping the wet ones on the laundry floor, he could hear voices from the kitchen. Dallas and Grandma and someone else, a male voice that he knew he'd heard somewhere before but couldn't quite place.

The house looked strange again, and its musty, catty smell made his hackles rise. What an unlikely thing to do, build a house, he thought. And then weigh it down with stuff, and anchor it to the earth with wires and pipes and sewers so there was no chance it would get away. Being inside made him uneasy, and he didn't want to talk to anyone, but he was really hungry.

"Is there anything left to eat?" he said, as he went into the kitchen.

Grandma was sitting at the table with the young policeman who had been at their house before, the one Tod thought of as Bullet Head.

"I kept something hot for you, though you don't deserve it," Dallas said in a bossy older sister voice. "Say hi to Rick and wash your hands."

"My rule used to be if you weren't on time for tea then you went hungry," Grandma observed.

"Sorry," Tod said. *Rick* he was thinking. How come she's calling him Rick? Sounds very friendly. He looked suspiciously at his sister. Her face was pink and her eyes unusually bright. And wasn't she wearing makeup? That wasn't like Dallas.

"Hi, Tod," Bullet Head said, cheerfully. "Bit late to be roaming around, isn't it? Been keeping out of trouble?"

"He doesn't get into trouble," Grandma put in quickly, sounding as if she were sorry for being cross before. "He's a good kid."

Tod was annoyed by this remark, as well as by Bullet Head Rick's patronizing tone. None of them knew anything about him. None of them would ever guess what had happened to him. There was a feeling between his older sister and the policeman he didn't like, a friendly tension as though they were about to embark on a new adventure together. He remembered he had to pass on Shaun's message to Charm, so without saying anything to anyone he left the kitchen and went to the girls' bedroom.

Charm was lying on her back on the bed with a black mask over her eyes and headphones over her ears. She was singing along to the tape in a soft moan, and her hands waved gently in time to the music. Tod watched her for a few minutes. There was something about her that made him feel sad and lonely. He couldn't work out what it was—something to do with how beautiful she'd become. He wished he were older—and someone else . . .

He threw Dallas's pillow at her. She sat up with a yell of rage, pulling the mask off.

"You little brat, what'd you do that for?"

Tod pulled the headphones off so she could hear him. "Lover boy Shaun is waiting outside for you! Just thought you'd like to know."

Charm stretched like a cat, and almost seemed to purr with pleasure. She got lazily up and went to the mirror. She gazed at her own face as though she were deeply in love with it. Then she brushed dark makeup on her eyes and put on some silver earrings which Tod knew were Leonie's. She sprayed perfume under her ears and down her front. The sweet, musky scent made Tod feel slightly sick, but it also excited him with its suggestion of nighttime adventures.

He followed Charm to the front door. "Can I come with you?" he said as she opened it.

"Don't be an idiot."

"What are you going to do?"

"I don't know. Just talk for a bit, I suppose." She went swiftly down the path. Tod watched from the front door. Shaun came out of the shadows to meet her, took her hand, and pulled her toward him. Tod wanted to carry on watching, but he wasn't sure he should. He slammed the door shut.

Things were even worse back in the kitchen. Dallas and Rick were carrying on as if they'd been friends for life. Tod felt as if he'd fallen asleep in a movie and missed a large chunk of the plot. When had they got so chummy and how come no one had told him? He ate as quickly as possible and went to bed.

When he got up the next morning everything looked supernormal. Had he just dreamed he had met the fox-man, Dan Russell? And been changed into a fox himself? But he felt a rippling feeling through his body that he recognized and surely he would never have dreamed up that name. . . .

The washing machine was rattling away in the laundry as he went past, and he could smell toast and coffee coming from the kitchen. Inkspot wound around and around his feet at the back door nearly tripping him. Outside he found Grandma hard at work in the vegetable garden.

"Perfect weather for planting," she called to Tod. "The soil's beautiful after the rain."

He could smell it, rich and earthy. The chooks were watching Grandma carefully, hoping she'd turn up some worms for them. Two magpies sang peacefully in the big gum tree at the back of the yard.

Everything was just as it usually was. Only he was no longer the same.

The front gate clicked, and from the steps he could just see Charm walk around the side of the house.

Grandma straightened up. "Crikey, girl," she shouted. "Have you been out all night?"

Charm jumped guiltily at the sound of her voice. "No!" she shouted back. "I've just been out for a walk." But when Tod followed her into the house, he noticed she was wearing the clothes she'd been in the previous night and the silver earrings. Beneath the perfume her hair smelled of cigarette smoke and something else. Another person's scent was mingled with her own.

Dallas only noticed the cigarette smoke when Charm went into the kitchen. She sniffed the air and said, "Have you been smoking?"

"No!" Charm took the jug of rainwater from the refrigerator and drank two glasses one after the other.

That's another lie, Tod thought, as he poured himself a glass of milk and added some cocoa to it. Dallas wasn't taken in by it either.

"Charm, you can't smoke, you get asthma."

"Who said I was smoking? Anyway, I haven't had asthma for years."

"You had an attack last year. You ended up in the hospital for two days! And where've you been all night?"

"That was in Sydney. The air's different here. I am not going to get asthma!" Charm banged her glass down on the drain board, and stormed out of the room. As she slammed the bathroom door she yelled back at Dallas, "Mind your own damn business."

"Gee," Dallas said. "She's in a vile mood. I'm going to tell Mum."

"Don't," Tod said. "Just mind your own business. It's nothing to do with you."

Dallas gave him a suspicious look. "You knew she was out all night, didn't you?"

Tod shrugged his shoulders and ate a slice of toast.

"Was she out with that boy—the one they think did the graffiti stuff?"

"How the hell should I know?"

"Rick says you shouldn't have anything to do with him. He says he's a real little scumbag. That's why I worry when you're out in the quarries. You might get hurt or into trouble. Rick says you should stay away from there."

"Rick says, Rick says," Tod mimicked her. "You sound as if you're in love with him!"

"Shut up," Dallas said. "Eat your breakfast and then come and help me hang out the washing before school."

Before Tod could finish his toast, Dallas yelled at him from the laundry.

"Come here!"

Her voice was furious. Whatever's wrong with her now? he wondered.

She was standing by the washing machine holding up the jeans he'd been wearing the night before. A few soggy bits of paper were clinging to the outside of the pocket.

"Oh no," Tod cried. "It was a letter from Dad."

Dallas pulled the rest of the letter from the pocket. It was in shreds, and the writing had run and blurred so that it was impossible to read.

"What did he say, Tod?"

"I don't know," Tod replied miserably. "I couldn't read his writing."

Dallas went on staring at the ruined letter. "You idiot! Didn't you think someone else might have wanted to read it? Why on earth didn't you leave it out so we'd see it? I've been waiting and waiting for another letter! You're impossible, Tod. You never think of anyone but yourself."

Tod couldn't remember Dallas ever yelling at him like that. She was the one who always protected him and stood up for him. She didn't need to be so angry, he thought. It was just a mistake. He stared back at her, furious.

To his horror he saw that she was crying, the tears rolling silently down her cheeks and dropping into the open washing machine. He felt terrible. He hadn't seen Dallas cry for years, not since she was in primary school and their cat was hit by a car. Charm cried all the time, tears of rage or despair or even sheer happiness, but never Dallas.

"Don't cry," he said, feeling guilty, and then angrier because he felt guilty. "I'm sorry, Dallas. Please don't cry."

Grandma came stumping into the house, whistling cheerfully, her hands covered in mud, her face streaked with it too. She came over to the tub to wash it off.

"Good grief," she said, taking a quick look at Dallas's face. "What's up with you, girl?"

"Don't touch me." Dallas sniffed, jumping back. "You'll put mud on my uniform, and it's the only one I've got." Then she cried even harder.

"Hold your horses," Grandma said. "I'll just wash my hands, and we'll sit down and have a nice cup of tea, and you can tell me what's bothering you, and then we'll sort it all out."

"It was my fault," Tod said. "There was a letter from Dad yesterday, and I put it in my pocket to read later, and it fell to pieces in the washing machine."

"It's not only the letter," Dallas said. She looked in each pocket for a tissue but couldn't find one, so she tried to dry her eyes on the laundry towel. "It's everything. The house being attacked. And Charm about to go off the rails again. She stayed out all night, Grandma. I wish Dad was here." She looked at Grandma with watery eyes. "Do you think he's ever going to come back? I wish Mum would talk about it, but she's so vague. And I think she likes it here. Sometimes I think she likes it better without him." Her eyes began to overflow again, and she grabbed at the towel which Grandma had taken to dry her hands on.

"There, there," Grandma said, patting her on the shoulder.

"Come on, I'll make you a cup of tea."

Once she started talking Dallas found she couldn't stop. "It's so unfair," she said, her hands cupped around the mug of strong tea Grandma had made for her. "I shouldn't have to worry about all this. I'm in my last year of school. I've got assignments and assessments all the time. I'm falling behind with my work. I never have time to do my homework. I'm never going to get the marks I need."

"You want me to wake Leonie up and tell her all this?" Grandma said.

Dallas shook her head. "No, she'll only be cranky. She hates getting up early. And there'll be a terrible row about Charm. I'd better make sure she gets to school, at least." She sniffed loudly and took a big gulp of tea. "And I'll be late if I don't get a move on."

"Dallas, your mother's already got a mother. Me! And I gave up trying to mother her years ago. She doesn't need you to look after her. She should be looking after you."

"I know, I know," Dallas said. Then her face crumpled up again. "I wish I'd been able to read Dad's letter. What are we going to do about that?"

"You can write to him and tell him it got lost," Grandma said briskly. "Or what about phoning him?"

Tod looked at her in amazement. Grandma never even used long distance. She must be feeling sorry for Dallas to suggest an international phone call.

"You could be doing something useful, Tod," she said now, returning his look with a stern one of her own. "Make yourself some lunch and get off to school. And try and stay out of trouble. We don't need any more of it." She gave Dallas another pat on the shoulder. "Don't worry, love," she said. "We're going to keep this family afloat. I haven't battled through this far to go under now. You go to school too and work hard. I'll look after things on the home front."

She got up with a determined look on her face and went to the bathroom. She thumped on the door and yelled out to Charm, "Charmian, my girl, come out of there. I want to have a word with you about how you behave when you're living in my house."

Charm refused to come out of the bathroom, and when Tod left for school Grandma was still hammering on the door. He wondered who would win that battle, and whose side he was on anyway. He still felt a bit snarly toward his family, especially Dallas who'd no right to yell at him like she did. He trotted through the reserve, swinging his head to catch the fresh morning smells. When he arrived in the school yard he was panting.

Martin raced up to him. "Are you all right? What happened to you yesterday? Why didn't you phone? I thought something awful must have happened. Mum was in a panic. She wanted to call the cops. But then Dad came home and said it wasn't really our business and that you were bound to be all right. So were you?"

Tod shrugged. It was impossible to put into words all that had happened to him since he had last seen Martin. They were living in two totally different worlds.

"So why didn't you phone?" Martin repeated.

"Didn't get home till late, and then I went to bed," Tod said. "It's no big deal, is it?"

"I thought you were coming over," Martin replied. "Mum made a cake and everything."

Tod didn't say anything. He could taste something in his mouth and it wasn't cake. He licked his lips at the thought of it, recollecting the springy sweet flesh. The fox thoughts began to swirl in his mind again. He heard very little of school lessons all day, but after lunch his class had art and Ms. Linkman told them they could paint anything they liked. As soon as Tod saw the big white sheet of paper in front of him, he saw the colors and shapes that should be on it. He hadn't known he could feel like that, as if the picture were deep inside him and had to be physically dragged out. He wasn't even sure what he was painting until he had finished, and Ms. Linkman stood behind him and said in a strange voice, "That's really good, Tod. Tell me about it."

He looked at the rippling shapes and the earth colors. He saw the fox patterns, the tip of the brush and the pointed ears. Behind the swirling shapes he could see Dan Russell's grin and his green eyes. He was quite pleased with what he saw. It wasn't exactly the same as he'd seen inside his head, but it was close. Next time he did it he would get closer. But he didn't want to share it with Ms. Linkman, or anyone else. "Oh, I don't know," he said vaguely. "It's just a picture."

"I'd like to put it up on the wall," she said, looking at it intently.

"I want to take it home," Tod said and added on the spur of the moment, "I'm going to send it to my dad."

He would write to Laurie and explain about the missing letter, and send him the picture. The thought made him very happy. As soon as he got home he went through Grandma's collection of old envelopes and Jiffy bags to try and find one big enough for the painting. Grandma got him some pieces of cardboard, too, to put it between so it wouldn't get bent in the post. Then Tod sat at the kitchen table with Dallas's Garfield notepaper and wrote to his father.

Dear Dad (Truck), I lost your letter. I'm sorry. Please write agian. I pianted this picture today. I miss you. Love from Tod.

He had been pleased with the painting, but he wasn't pleased with the letter at all. He wanted to tell Dad about the quarries and the fox, about Charm and Shaun, and Dallas yelling because the washing machine chewed up Laurie's letter, and about Rick, who had patted her on the shoulder, and about the way Mum seemed to be disappearing out of his life. There were so many things that Dad needed to know about, but it was far too hard to put them all into words and write them down. He looked at the notepaper, depressed. Even Garfield couldn't make him smile. He wondered if he should start again, but the task seemed too daunting. *PS,* he added at the bottom of the sheet, *Please come home.*

He stuck the letter to the outside of the cardboard with some Sellotape and sealed up the Jiffy bag. Grandma promised she would post it in the morning when she went to the shops.

The phone rang and Leonie answered it. "That's very kind of you," Tod heard her say, "I'll just ask him." She put her head around the kitchen door. "There's someone called Mrs. Hall on the phone," she whispered. "Says you're a friend of her son, Matthew."

"Martin," Tod said.

"Martin, whatever. They want you to stay with them this weekend. It's his birthday. Shall I tell them you're busy? She sounds a bit of a pain!"

"Can't I go?" Tod said.

"Of course you can go if you want to. I just thought you might find it a bit dull. She sounds a very boring woman."

Tod didn't want Leonie to make decisions for him or make judgments about his friends and their mothers. "Mum," he remonstrated, "she's nice."

"Okay, okay, I'll say you can go." Leonie rolled her eyes

dramatically at Tod and disappeared again. Tod heard her voice, artificially pleasant, saying again how kind it was of them and Tod would simply love to. He was suddenly really angry with the way she was always acting. He was glad she didn't know about Dan Russell or Shaun Stone and the Breakers, glad she hadn't seen the picture, glad she knew so little about him.

He went to bed and wondered when Dan Russell would come for him. He hoped it would be soon. He couldn't wait to be a fox again.

ELEVEN

Inkspot slept on Tod's bed every night now. He moved onto Grandma's bed in the daytime. It was cooler in the main part of the house. Tod's little lean-to was becoming unbearable as the weather grew warmer. The cat slept most of the time, only waking up for meals and a short stalk outside around the garden.

"Poor old cat," Grandma said. "He must be twelve or thirteen years old. I wonder how much longer he'll last."

"You should get another cat," Tod said. "Or a dog," he added hopefully.

Grandma smiled. "I'd love to, but I don't think I should. I can't help worrying about what would happen to them after I've gone."

"But that won't be for ages, Grandma," Tod exclaimed.

"Well, I hope not, but you never know, not when you get to my age."

Sitting on his bed a few nights later, stroking Inkspot, Tod thought about this. He couldn't bear the idea of the old cat not being there anymore—and the idea of Grandma dying was terrible. Still, Grandma had lived a lot longer than Inkspot. It was really unfair that animals had such short lives.

He put out the light and lay in bed listening to the sounds from the rest of the house. One by one they stopped. Everyone went to bed except Charm, who was out somewhere with Shaun. He could hear the sounds of the night through the open windows. A train went by up the hill—he guessed it was the 10:33. It was hard to sleep with the moon shining full and bright outside, but the house was completely silent. No one else was awake. They were deep, deep asleep.

Deep in the fox sleep.

Tod leaped out of bed and ran to the back door. Grandma had left it open to let the cool night air into the house. Through the screen Tod could see the dark shape of the big fox.

He felt a sense of urgency and impatience. He saw the night waiting for him.

Dan Russell's green eyes were bright in the moonlight and full of power.

Tod stepped out into the night. He dropped on all fours as the screen door slammed behind him. He felt his skin ripple and swirl. His head flattened and his face sharpened. His ears twitched and became pointed. The power ran through his spine and limbs, suppling and strengthening them. He opened his mouth and passed his tongue over his sharp teeth. He grinned at Dan Russell and his tail swung from side to side.

He was aware of the tantalizing smell of the poultry from the run on the hill, and the infuriating smell of cat around the house. The fur rose on the back of his neck. He knew Dan Russell felt the same about cats.

Bad.

The two foxes touched noses.

Hunting.

They padded down the concrete path along the side of the

house. Tod's nose twitched as they passed the sewerage cover and he caught the smell of drains.

Dan Russell flattened himself on his belly to squeeze under the gate. Tod imitated him. He was surprised at how flexible his fox self was, more like a cat than a dog. He could flatten himself until he was almost two dimensional. And he was pleased with how quietly he trotted up the street after Dan Russell, keeping to the shadows, almost invisible.

They crossed the railway and followed the track, not up the hill as Tod would have expected, but down the hill toward the city.

Tod could see perfectly in the moonlight. From his new low viewpoint the houses looked huge and their fences made impossible barriers. From behind the fences came all sorts of enticing smells. He was terribly hungry.

Dan Russell knew every house and yard. Some they went past without stopping. Tod noted a strong smell, not as irritating as the cat smell, but one to avoid.

Dog.

At one house they crawled through a hole under the fence made by a cat, and found dried cat food left in a bowl outside the back door. The smell of cat made Tod wrinkle up his nose, but it was worth it to crunch up the pellets. The foxes pushed each other out of the way to get at the food bowl and then lapped from the water bowl next to it.

In another yard the gate had fallen off its hinges. The yard was messy and full of weeds, and a delicious smell came from the back where some bones had been buried in a compost heap. The two foxes dug them up and gnawed on them, cracking them open with their strong white teeth. Then they sat for a long time outside a tumbledown garden shed. There was a strong and interesting smell, and Tod could hear rustling and squeaking from inside. He didn't move until something suddenly ran out under the door and then without thinking he pounced, snapped, and swallowed. He had eaten a mouse and it was the best thing he'd ever tasted, much better than the cat food or the bones.

Dan Russell laughed silently.

Good.

Tod licked his lips and watched eagerly for another one.

Dan Russell got to his feet and stretched.

Hunting.

They trotted back up the railway line, leaving the quiet suburban houses behind them. All their occupants seemed to be wrapped in the deep fox sleep. The foxes hadn't seen or heard a single human while they were on the prowl, though they couldn't help but smell them. Now the human smell lessened a little. Soon Tod could pick up the distinctive smell of the depot, diesel from the trucks and machines and a garbagey whiff from the dump behind, together with fresh dug earth and rotting garden refuse. Despite the cat food, the bones, and the mouse, he was still hungry, with the deep gnawing hunger he'd felt so often lately.

His teeth ached with hunger. He wanted to bite something.

Dan Russell knew. Tod could sense him laughing. The big fox flicked his brush cheerfully as he led Tod off the track and into the little reserve where the boy had buried the dead fox so many months ago. The moon, low in the sky now, lit up the drying grass and cast twisted shadows from the big gum trees. From the creek bed came a clamor of frog voices. Insects chirped and a night bird made a throaty croaking call.

Down by the creek the grass was still green and damp. Dan Russell munched on a few stems and Tod did the same, but they did nothing to still the pangs of hunger. The earth smelled of mint and mud and decay—life and death all mixed up together—and the smell and his hunger and the moonlight filled him with a sort of madness.

He rubbed his muzzle in the mud, and then lay and rolled in it. It felt cool and delicious. He rolled over and jumped at Dan Russell. The big fox feinted sideways. Tod jumped and missed again. Then he leaped into the air, and when his paws touched the ground again he ran for the sheer joy of running. Dan Russell chased him. Soundlessly they ran, twisting and turning, now one, now the other fleeing and following.

With no one to watch, the foxes danced and played in the moonlight, until the sky began to pale in the east.

Dan Russell turned abruptly and padded along the creek bed.

Rabbit time.

Tod followed. They were both panting. They stopped to drink from a deeper pool where the concrete drain led under the railway track. Then they entered the drain and ran through it, underneath the depot.

Once out the other side the big fox's demeanor changed again. He was no longer playful but deadly serious. Tod still wanted to run, but when he tried to push past, Dan Russell showed his teeth and blocked him with his shoulder.

Play over. Hunting.

They crept like shadows along the creek, following it to where the ash trees grew. Long before they had reached the spot, Tod could smell what they were after, the best smell so far.

Rabbit.

The gully wind was freshening and it blew the rabbit smell toward them, blowing their own scent down the hill, away from the rabbits, which were grazing on the grass that still grew green under the ash trees.

Stay.

Dan Russell disappeared. Tod dropped onto his haunches, quivering with excitement and hunger, unable to take his eyes off the feeding rabbits. There were half a dozen or so of them. They nibbled with quick, neat movements, and every few minutes sat up and looked around, their long ears and delicate noses twitching constantly. He could see the huge dark pupils of their eyes. Their smell was driving him mad.

He couldn't see Dan Russell at all, but suddenly his nose told him where the other fox was. He had circled around behind the rabbits. In the same instant, the rabbits caught the fox smell too. They scattered and ran—but one of them ran straight toward Tod. He didn't need to think. He pounced. The rabbit saw him and swerved, leaping and twisting away from him. Faster than thought he followed it, just like in his dream. The smell of it filled his brain. It was right in front of him. It was his. He snapped and shook. The rabbit shrieked once and went limp in his mouth. Through the fur he could taste blood.

Dan Russell came trotting up, his teeth bared in a grin.

Good.

Tod was crunching the rabbit's head. He drew back a little so Dan Russell could eat too. Dan Russell tore a leg off the carcass and gnawed at it.

By the time the foxes had finished eating and there was nothing left of the rabbit but scattered fur, the sky was light and the sun about to rise. Now he was no longer so hungry, Tod realized how tired he was. He wanted to find somewhere dark and cool to stretch out away from the sun. In his mind he saw Dan Russell's den in the mysterious quarry. He thought it would be nice to go there and lie down for the day, and then go hunting again at night. Dimly alongside this picture he saw another one—a picture of a boy in a bedroom inside a human house. With a jolt of surprise he remembered the boy was him.

Home.

Dan Russell looked at him with his fierce green eyes. They held the same dangerous look Tod had seen before. He knew if he wanted to—and Dan Russell did want him to—he could stay a fox forever, and always live in a fox's clear-cut, exciting, immediate world. As their eyes locked for a moment Tod saw in them everything that could be his—the animal life, connected to the earth, flowing on, year after year, century after century, being part of the whole earth, not disconnected and alienated from it. He saw the harsh fox life, with its brevity and pain, but he saw that the pain was not like human pain. It was purely physical. It did not tear at the heart or torment the mind. And it was short, and after it came death, but death was just a diving back into the earth, the eater becoming the eaten, feeding as well as being fed.

Home.

Not yet, not yet.

Dan Russell gave him a look as if he knew exactly what was passing through Tod's mind. He licked his paws and then began to trot up the hill away from the creek toward the quarries. After a moment's hesitation Tod followed, finding it hard to keep up with the steady pace. His muscles had started to ache, and his paws were sore.

Halfway up the hill Dan Russell halted suddenly and Tod nearly ran into him from behind. The wind had dropped a little, but it was still blowing in their faces and on it was a strong rank smell. Tod saw Dan Russell's hackles rise and his white-tipped brush grow thicker and more bushy. He felt his own do the same.

There was a smell of food on the wind too, something fresh

killed and bloody. His mouth started to water. Dan Russell began to pace cautiously up the track. Tod bounded less cautiously after him.

Ahead of them they heard a fiendish scream. It stopped both foxes dead. Their ears flattened and they showed their teeth.

Cat.

Dan Russell sniffed the air. Ahead of them on the track was by far the biggest cat Tod had ever seen, huge and tabby striped, with a broad flat skull and tattered ears lying close to its head. Its eyes were yellow and fierce and it was showing its teeth in a snarl. It looked like a small tiger. It crouched, claws unsheathed, over a dead bird. It had been halfway through eating, and the bird's chest was torn open.

The cat screamed again at the foxes.

Tod didn't like the look of the cat's claws and the teeth, but he was curious about the bird. It smelled delicious. Not as good as rabbit, maybe, but good enough to start him feeling the savage hunger again. He was tired and his paws were sore. Catching rabbits was hard work. Surely it would be much easier to steal the cat's prey from it.

Dan Russell didn't seem to be doing anything, so Tod pushed past him and lunged for the dead bird. The cat gave an earsplitting yowl and lashed at him. Its claws raked the side of his muzzle making him yelp with surprise and pain. He jumped back, yipping. The cat took advantage of his discomfort, picked up the bird in its mouth, and, growling all the time, walked backward off the path and into the tangled kangaroo thorn bushes.

Pain. Fear.

Dan Russell wasn't laughing, as Tod half expected. His tail lashed in rage, and his hackles stayed up in anger. He even trotted in an angry and upset way. The smell of the cat was strong on the path and it made him snarl.

Anger. Hate.

Cat too strong.

Tod wondered if he meant the cat they had just seen or the cat spirit—presumably the cats had their own guardian spirit just like everything else. Dan Russell seemed to have lost face in some way in the encounter. He no longer seemed quite so powerful and all-knowing. Tod's muzzle hurt from the scratch and he couldn't reach it to lick it. He wanted his hands back.

Home.

Dan Russell turned to him, still angry. His eyes flashed, and in an instant Tod was standing on the hill in his human shape again. Without turning to say good-bye Dan Russell raced up the hill and disappeared into the undergrowth.

Tod had chosen to become human again but, as the excitement of the night began to fade, he felt like crying with disappointment. Daylight had come completely and the sun was almost over the rim of the hill. The thought of the coming glare and heat made him wince. He was exhausted and his face smarted from the cat's scratches. He touched them carefully. They were bleeding.

He wiped his face with his pajama sleeve. Jeez, he was outside in his *pajamas.* He fervently hoped no one would see him. He'd better get a move on before the workmen arrived at the depot. His feet were sore and he had no shoes. Limping over the rocky ground he painfully made his way home.

TWELVE

It was nearly half past six when Tod came around the side of the house. The chooks and ducks caught a glimpse of him and started their morning cackle.

He willed them to shut up, wanting to get into the house without anyone seeing him. He had no idea how he'd explain where he'd been all night. But before he could reach the back door, he heard a noise from the shed. He stopped and listened carefully. He heard someone whisper, heard a stifled laugh. He wrinkled his nose. There was a curious smell too. Cigarette smoke, mixed with something chemical—turps, that was it. He cautiously went to the door and peeped in.

Shaun and Charm were cleaning paint off their hands with Grandma's turpentine and some old rags. They both jumped guiltily when they saw Tod in the doorway.

"What are you doing?" Charm hissed at him. "Spying on us?"

"I'm not spying," Tod retorted. "I just wanted to know who was in here. You might have been burglars."

"Nothing worth nicking in here," Shaun said, carefully wiping a smudge of paint from Charm's eyebrows. He touched the spot he had just cleaned with his lips. "You smell gross," he said.

She started to laugh, and then began coughing. "So do you," she spluttered. "So does everything." Then she had to stop talking to cough some more.

"Are you okay?" Tod said. Charm had had asthma at school last year. He'd only heard about the attack afterward but he had a faint earlier recollection of waking up one night when he was about eight, and finding the house full of ambulancemen, and Charm gasping for breath with a mask over her face. It had scared him half to death, and the memory scared him now.

She got her breath and nodded. "Sure."

"What have you been doing?" he couldn't help asking.

"Painting," Charm boasted.

"You wouldn't help me," Shaun said. "So I had to do it myself." His face was flushed and his eyes bright with excitement.

"And I had to help him," Charm put in. She sounded very wheezy and she was holding her hands to her chest.

Tod felt a swift pang of disappointment and jealousy. He knew he'd told Shaun he didn't want to do the painting—but all the same he would have liked to have been asked again. Maybe he would have changed his mind, maybe he would have said yes. When he'd refused he didn't know Charm would go and help Shaun instead. He'd thought he was the only person outside all night, having daring adventures—but Charm had been out all night too, with Shaun, and they had been doing something possibly much more daring.

"So what's it like?" he demanded. He hoped it was terrible. He was pretty sure it would be. He could see so clearly within his mind what he would have painted up at the edge.

"It's cool," Charm said, and wheezed again.

"It's there," Shaun added. "That's the main thing. I don't care if it's good or not. What the hell does 'good' mean anyway? No one's going to give me any awards for it. No one's going to hang it in an art gallery. It's not going to get me an A for art. But it's there. It says 'I exist.' He dabbed at Charm's neck. "You're clean now, girl. You wanna check me over?"

She took the bottle of turps from him and started wiping his hands carefully. They were a nice shape, Shaun's hands, capable looking and strong, but the nails were bitten down to the quick, and there was a self-made tattoo of a cross in a circle on the back of the right hand and a chain pattern like a bracelet around the wrist.

Shaun bent his head and let Charm's hair hide his face.

"Hey," she said. "I can't see what I'm doing!"

"Disappear, kid," Shaun said to Tod.

"And for heaven's sake don't wake anyone else up," Charm added. "The last thing I want is the old dingbat having a stress attack at us."

Tod could hear her coughing as he went into the house. He was going to jump straight into bed and try and sleep before the hot sun on the roof of the lean-to woke him, but as he was pulling back the sheet he heard footsteps running and someone hammering on the back door.

Thought they didn't want to wake anyone up, he grumbled to himself as he went back to open it.

Shaun's face was white and scared. There were tears in his eyes and he was stammering.

"Something's wrong with Charm. I don't think she can breathe."

Tod ran back to the shed. Charm was leaning over the workbench, clawing at her chest. The turps had fallen from her hands and spilled on the floor. The fumes were terrible.

"What is it? What's wrong with her?" Shaun kept saying.

Tod dragged his sister into the fresh air, amazed through his alarm at how thin and frail she was. She was fighting to breathe. Her lips had gone blueish and her eyes were dark. She was making horrible sounds.

He remembered the ambulancemen.

"Shaun," he said, loudly, "I'm going to call for help. Stay here with her."

"I don't know what to do," Shaun said, panicking.

"Just stay calm and keep her calm. I've got to get help."

Charm's eyes turned to him, but she couldn't speak. Her hands reached out to him, but he tore himself away and ran into the house, shouting as he went.

"Dallas, Grandma, wake up, wake up!" He banged on the doors as he went past, hurting his hands but not really noticing. He grabbed the phone and dialed. His breath was coming in huge sobs so he could hardly speak.

Grandma was first out of her room.

"Get Charm," he shouted to her over the phone. "She's outside. She's having an asthma attack."

"God in heaven," Grandma exclaimed, stumbling down the passageway. Tod heard her swear as she stubbed her toe on the tea chest by the laundry room.

"Tod, what's happening?" Dallas was next out, her hair all over her face and her eyes puffy with sleep.

"Ambulance," he said, handing over the phone. "Tell them where to come. Tell them to hurry. It's Charm. She can't breathe."

"Go and wake Mum," Dallas said swiftly.

Leonie was still fast asleep on the sofa. The room smelled of cigarette smoke and her perfume. The rose-pink kimono was slung over the back of the sofa, glowing faintly in the morning light. Leonie's clothes from the night before were in a heap on the floor. Tod tripped over her shoes and nearly fell on top of her. Her eyes opened slightly and she peered at him, not quite awake.

"Toddy," she groaned. "It's way too early. . . ."

"Get up, Mum, Charm's sick. She can't breathe."

"Oh, my God." Leonie grabbed the kimono and wrapped it around herself as she struggled to her feet. She ran heavily to the back of the house and pushed through the screen door, clumsy with fear. Tod followed her.

Outside, Leonie turned to him. "Turn the shower on. Get the water really hot. Put the kettle on too. We need steam."

Tod went to do it, just catching a glimpse of Charm lying on the grass. Grandma was bending over her, breathing into her mouth. Charm's body looked limp, as limp as the rabbit and the bird. Waves of terror for her shuddered through him. Surely Charm couldn't be going to die?

Dallas was just putting the phone down.

"They're on their way," she said. "Shouldn't be more than a few minutes."

"Mum said steam," Tod told her briefly. "You do the kettle." He went into the bathroom and turned the shower on full. Lucky it's summer, he thought irrelevantly. Won't matter that there's no hot water later. He went to the kitchen. Dallas had filled the kettle and left it to boil. Tod leaned over it, willing it to hurry up. It seemed to take forever. He tore back to the bathroom. It wasn't very steamy—too big and drafty, and the window had never closed properly.

Don't let Charm die, he was praying. Don't let Charm die.

He thought of his father. Charm couldn't die while Laurie was away on the other side of the world. It couldn't happen.

The kettle still wasn't boiling when he went back to the kitchen.

He went outside again, dreading what he would find.

Charm was sitting up now, leaning against her mother. Her breathing was labored—but she was breathing. Her eyes were closed, and her face white.

"We'll take her inside," Leonie said to Grandma. "Sit her in the bathroom till the ambulance gets here."

"It should be here any minute," Dallas said, helping lift her sister. "It's okay," she said, seeing Tod's face. "She's going to be all right."

"Take her clothes off," Grandma said. "They reek of turps."

"Don't you dare take my clothes off," Charm said weakly. She was still protesting when they sat her on the chair in the bathroom as close to the steamy shower as possible. "For heaven's sake, it was bad enough getting the kiss of life from Grandma. Now you're going to drown me!"

"Sshh, sshh, baby, don't fret," Leonie said, speaking soothingly as if to a three year old. "Here, we'll wrap you up in this." She took off her pink kimono, and undid Charm's jeans. Taking her daughter's clothes off she helped her into the robe.

"I reckon she's feeling better," Grandma said. "Is that kettle boiling, Tod? You can make us a cup of tea." She pressed her hand to her chest and took a couple of deep breaths. "My heart's hammering away like an express train."

"What happened to Shaun?" Tod said as he and Grandma went into the kitchen.

"I sent him packing. Standing around like a wart, getting in the way. Fat lot of bloody use he was. Nearly killed the girl and all he can do is stand there and shake and look like he's going to start bawling."

She pulled a chair out from the kitchen table and sank

down in it, sighing heavily. "I don't know what those two were up to, but they're not getting away with it. I'm getting on to the police about them."

Before Tod could reply, the street filled with the sound of the siren as the ambulance turned the corner.

Charm was taken away to the hospital in the ambulance. Dallas went with her and Leonie followed in the Citröen, leaving Grandma and Tod at home. Grandma made Tod a big breakfast, which he thought he wouldn't be able to eat, but once he tasted the eggs and bacon he bolted them down. Then she wanted him to help her in the garden, before it got too hot, she said, but it was already unbearably hot, with a dry, fiery heat and a northerly wind.

They watered the vegetable garden and spread sacks over the lettuces, fed the poultry and filled up the ducks' tub. Then they retreated indoors. Grandma hung wet sheets over the screen doors, front and back, to try to cool the house.

"I reckon I'll clean out the kitchen cupboards," she said. "It's a good chance to do some indoor jobs, a day like this. And when you've had a bit of a shock it's not a bad idea to do something constructive. Takes your mind off things."

Tod groaned. He was so tired he could hardly keep his eyes open. Grandma gave him a sharp look.

"You're yawning your head off, boy. Couldn't you sleep last night? The moon kept you awake, I suppose."

"Something like that." Tod yawned again.

"I slept so deep it might have been a fox sleep," Grandma said, getting the stepladder out from behind the door. After a pause she said sharply, "So what happened to your face?"

Tod had forgotten the cat scratches. He put his hand up and felt them now. The blood had dried and scabs were forming.

"Inkspot scratched me," he said.

"First time he's ever scratched anyone," Grandma retorted. "What the heck did you do to him?" When Tod didn't answer she went on, "I hope you weren't out doing that graffiti stuff."

Tod shook his head. Grandma was looking at him closely as though she suspected him of lying.

"I thought you had more sense," she said.

Tod felt he'd lost her approval suddenly. He was too tired to care much.

"Charm's going to be okay, isn't she?" he said, partly to change the subject.

"Course, she is," Grandma said snappily. "She's got nine lives, that girl. She's a survivor. She'll always be all right. She'll just leave havoc and mayhem all round her. Probably be the death of her mother and me. Just wish she'd give that hooligan the flick."

She set the stepladder up with a forceful push. "Can you climb up on this and do the top shelves for me, Tod? I'll get the bucket and cloth."

"Grandma," he pleaded, "do I have to?"

"Won't hurt you to help," she replied tartly. She opened the cupboard doors and five or six tiny moths flew out.

"There," she exclaimed, swatting at them. "This really needs doing."

Tod climbed reluctantly to the top of the ladder and started passing jars and packets down to his grandmother. She sorted them out on the table, emptying some that were full of moths into the chook bucket, and lining the rest up in rows.

"What on earth is in this?" Tod said, holding up an ancient Bushells coffee jar. "They look like dried ears!"

"Oh, they're the apricots I dried last year." Grandma chuckled. "I was wondering what happened to them." She opened the jar and popped one into her mouth.

"Take the cloth and wipe the shelf," she mumbled to Tod through the apricot.

He wiped away vigorously, but he hadn't noticed a jar in the corner. The cloth caught it and dragged it to the edge. Both Grandma and Tod tried to catch it. Tod's nails caught Grandma on the wrist. Grandma's hand knocked Tod off the stepladder. He landed on the table. The jar fell on the floor and smashed. The table tipped sideways. Tod slid onto the floor, followed by Grandma's rows of jars and the chook bucket.

"Crikey," Grandma spluttered, nearly choking on the apricot. "You silly thing! Have you hurt yourself?"

"I don't think so," Tod said, wiping a mixture of lentils and flour off his knees.

"Don't move, don't move," Grandma cried. "There's broken glass everywhere. I don't want you to cut yourself. Crikey, that's a mess and a half you managed to make." She surveyed the scene glumly. "I'll have to sweep up around you. Hold still for a minute while I get the broom."

When she'd swept up the glass, she pulled Tod to his feet, gave him a whack on the bum, and said, "Go on, get out of here. I think I'll manage better on my own."

"Sorry, Grandma," he said, feeling about three years old as he went out of the kitchen.

The house was baking. The sheets on the screen doors were already almost dry. Tod went outside and got the hose. He washed the rest of the flour off himself, and sprayed the sheets again. The water was running out warm, but he wet his head under it and it made him feel cooler.

He didn't want to go back inside again. He wanted to sleep desperately, but he'd never get to sleep with Grandma crashing around, and anyway there was nowhere cool enough. He remembered the night before. How lovely the mud had felt on his fox muzzle. The creek would be the coolest place to be, under the ash trees or even underground in the storm-water drain.

He got his sneakers from his room, gave Inkspot a quick stroke and told him he was sorry for lying about him, and went out into the stifling street.

The air was harsh and dusty. The wind whipped at the gum trees and blew grit into his eyes. There was no one around. It was one of those one-hundred-degree days when everyone stayed home with their air conditioners on, unless they had old-fashioned grandmothers who didn't hold with using electricity unnecessarily and who draped wet sheets over their doors instead.

Grandma was okay. She'd probably saved Charm's life. She hadn't panicked at all, just kept her breathing until the ambulancemen arrived with the oxygen. He wondered if she would report Charm to the police, and what would happen then. Another little visit from Bullet Head, no doubt. Well, Dallas would love that!

The patches of mud in the creek bed had shrunk since the night before. Tod looked at the paw marks in them. He recognized his own small fox prints and Dan Russell's bigger ones. It made him feel weird, as though he were looking through a peephole into another world. Despite the hot wind, he shivered. His skin crawled. He couldn't help remembering the rabbit. He'd killed it. Part of him was horrified, but another, stronger part couldn't wait to go hunting again.

He peered into the storm-water drain. It looked dark and cool inside. He sniffed. He could distinctly smell a trace of fox. He dropped on all fours and crawled through the drain, scraping his head on the roof a couple of times before he remembered he was much larger than he had been when he was a fox.

His human eyesight was not nearly as good either, especially after the brightness outside, so he didn't see the bag until he tripped over it. He felt down to see what he'd stumbled over, picked it up, and carried it down to the far end to take a better look at it in the light.

It was some kind of army surplus kit bag, made of khaki canvas, lined with a dark green rubbery material. Inside were several spray cans and tubes of paint—black, gray, silver, purple, and orange. Tod inspected them carefully, whistling soundlessly through his teeth.

He wondered exactly where the rest of the paint was, the paint that had been in the cans and tubes and was now somewhere along the railway line. Once it was just an object, bought—or more likely nicked—off a shelf in a shop, but now it had been turned into something else, into a part of Shaun Stone. It had taken on a life of its own. Probably right now people would be looking at it as the trains they were in went up and down the hill. It would be saying things to people as they either admired or deplored it.

Thinking about all this, he put the paints carefully back again, and left the coolness of the drain. He wanted to take a look at what the paints had turned into for himself.

Outside it was growing hotter by the minute. The quarry area was like a furnace. It felt as if it would burst into flames at any moment. The air no longer seemed like air but like an altogether different substance. He wondered how the foxes, with their thick European coats, had coped with such temperatures when they first arrived. He could feel their terror on the journey, trapped in tiny cages on a boat that rolled and heaved for months. Then being released into a completely alien landscape, where even the stars were strange. Nothing smelled the same, nothing looked the same. The only familiar things were the white humans and the livestock they'd brought with them.

How clever the foxes were, Tod thought. It was clever of them to survive so far from their natural home. Of course, they had Dan Russell to look after them. The thought made him smile.

He followed the track up the hill. The hot air burned his throat, and dried his sweat immediately. Apart from the northerly wind rattling the trees, it was very quiet. Even the birds were silenced by the heat. Tod dropped on all fours again to climb the steepest part of the slope, and then began to make his way through the undergrowth toward the railway line.

Through the trees he caught a gleam of something on the largest concrete slab near the tunnel. Something was painted on it in purple and silver, with strong black outlines. Coming closer he could see all Shaun's piece, high above the track, clearly visible from the trains. It wouldn't have been easy to paint. He was amazed Shaun had managed it in a single night—but of course Charm had been there to help.

He studied the piece dispassionately. It was nothing special—swirls of silver and black around the big purple letters: SS. And there was too much orange added around the edges. The lettering was hurried and boring. It might have looked all right closer to the city, but out here, surrounded by rocks and trees, it looked silly.

He could have done something much better. Something that belonged in this place, but that was also part of him.

He could hear a train coming up the hill. He drew back under cover of the bushes. He didn't want anyone to see him or to think the painting was his. As he shrank back, making himself into a silent, watchful part of the landscape, he became aware of someone else nearby. He could smell him.

Shaun was standing a few yards away, partly shielded from anyone below by the trunk of a gum tree. He had a knife in his hand, and while Tod watched he stabbed it into the tree a couple of times. He had seen Tod, but he didn't say anything until the train had disappeared into the tunnel. Then he said, "Is she okay?"

"Grandma says she will be," Tod replied. The asthma attack seemed distant and unreal now, blurred by his tiredness after the fox adventure.

"I thought she was going to die," Shaun said, his lisping voice sounding more childlike than usual. He shifted position awkwardly and looked away, rubbing the side of his face and blinking

"What made you disappear like that?" Tod said quietly.

"I thought she was going to die," Shaun said again. "And I didn't know what to do. I was just standing there in the way. The old woman told me to get going. Said she was calling the police about us. Do you think she means it?"

"Probably," Tod said. "The police know all about you already anyway. It's not going to make much difference."

"They've never taken me to court yet," Shaun said with a slight grin. "But they might this time."

"You worried?"

"Nah. Courts won't do anything. Just tell you you're a naughty boy and not to do it again." Shaun laughed shortly. "It's all a game, see. You see how far you can get, they see how far they can get. Life would be bloody boring for everyone if people like me weren't around." He stabbed the tree again, then drew out the knife and held it up to Tod. The blade caught the sun, blinding him for a second.

"This is what life is like," Shaun said. "It's like the blade of a knife, and you're trying to keep your balance on it. If it tilts and you have to grab hold—you cut yourself." He turned the knife over and gripped the sharp edge with his other hand. When he opened up his palm there was a thin line of blood right across it.

"Life's sharp. It cuts you." He licked the blood away with his tongue. Tod felt his own mouth water.

"So what do you think of the piece?" Shaun said, unable to hide his pride in it. "Sorry you weren't part of it now?"

A freight train was lumbering up the hill, three green engines pulling a long line of flatbeds laden with containers. By the time it reached the tunnel it was almost as slow as walking speed. The noise echoed back from the sides of the embankment, and it saved Tod from having to answer Shaun. When the last flatbed had disappeared into the tunnel, the older boy spoke again, darting on to something else.

"You could ride on them, you know. You could jump onto the trains easily just before the tunnel. People do it in films all the time. Then you'd get out of this dump. Get away from here."

He gazed toward the dark tunnel. They could hear the train hooting from the other side.

"There's never any caboose," Shaun went on. "They read us a book in school when I was a kid about the little red caboose. I liked that story. I like trains. But there never is a little red caboose." He looked at Tod. "Why is that, d'you know?"

His voice was artless. Tod could see suddenly the child he'd been—still was really—for all his swaggering, his guns, and his macho-man attitude.

"Books are always telling you things that aren't true," Tod

said, remembering the stories of the foxes that wore clothes. "That's why I don't like them much."

"You don't read too good, do you? I remember now, Adrian told me. You'll never make it in high school if you can't read." He looked pityingly at Tod. "But don't worry. I'll look out for you. No one'll dare hassle you."

Tod didn't reply. He didn't like to think about high school. It loomed ahead as dark as the mouth of the tunnel on the train track below them. There was something comforting about the fact that Shaun would be looking out for him there. He would have a group to belong to. He remembered his earlier fantasy about taking on the Breakers. Now it seemed like a rather silly and childish dream.

Shaun had squatted down and was tracing patterns in the dirt with the point of the knife. The air shimmered in the heat. Tod's throat was dry with thirst. He was thinking he should go home when from below came another noise, not loud enough to be a train. A State Transport Authority truck was coming slowly up the track that ran along the side of the rails. It stopped as close to the painting as it could get and two men got out.

"Shit, it's the bloody buff!" Shaun exclaimed.

The men put ladders up against the concrete slab, and started to spray.

"Damn them. Damn them," Shaun kept saying over and over again as he watched his piece disappear section by section under the thick green paint. He was shaking with rage and frustration, and almost sobbing.

"They won't win," he said finally, more in control, when the buff was almost finished. "I'll do it again. They're not going to stop me. They can't wipe me out that easily. I'll just get out there and do another one."

He turned to Tod, and grabbed him by the arm. "And you're going to help me this time, aren't you? Promise you will! We'll do a piece that's so bloody terrific no one'll ever want to buff it."

Shaun's grip was so strong he was hurting Tod, and he still held the knife in his other hand. But it wasn't fear that made Tod nod his head. It was a mixture of all sorts of things: pleasure that Shaun had asked him again, anger at the men below wiping out what Shaun had done, a desire not to be treated like a kid anymore, wanting to be part of a gang that included Charm.

"Okay," he said. "Get me the paints and I'll do it."

THIRTEEN

Charm stayed in the hospital for the next two days, so she missed going to hear Leonie at the Lion on Sunday night.

"I want you all to come and support me," Leonie had said. "I'm really getting better, and I think I'm finally getting somewhere. This is going to be the biggest gig I've had yet and I'd love my family to be there for me."

She put on her devoted-mother voice which was hard to resist. Grandma said she wasn't going to go and watch her make a fool of herself, but Dallas and Tod couldn't get out of it. Rick said he wouldn't miss it for the world, and offered to drive them.

"You were lucky," Tod told Charm the next day when she was home from the hospital. He'd found her after school lying on the bed in his room. There had been a mild southerly change the night before, so it was a little cooler, but Tod could feel the heat building up again.

Charm looked even paler than usual, but her breathing was back to normal. She was meant to be resting, but she kept jumping off the bed and prowling around Tod's room, picking Tod's things up, looking at them, and then dropping them on the floor.

"I would have died of embarrassment." She groaned,

kicking his schoolbag out of the way. "It must have been awful!"

"She pointed us out at the start," Tod said. "Everyone knew we were her family. And they kept turning around to look at us when she made jokes about us."

"What exactly did she say?"

"Everything! Our whole lives. Like 'I told my husband to get lost once too often and he's gone away to find himself.' One daughter going out with a cop and the other with a graffiti vandal. Something about the whole drama of life going on in the kitchen. Even you getting asthma from the turps— she made it sound like a huge joke!"

Charm grinned. "It was a bit of a joke if you're into black humor."

"Didn't feel funny to me," Tod replied grimly. "And then she kept making weak puns like . . . what was it? . . . how she didn't miss her husband, she hit him fair and square, and the only thing they had in common is they were married on the same day."

"I suppose it is a bit pathetic," Charm said.

"And she said teenagers were nature's way of making sure people grow old—that's why they're called agers, because they age you—and they work as a team, so it really should be teamagers. The Thirty-sixers. All sorts of stuff like that. And you should have seen what she looked like!"

"What did she wear?"

"It was what she didn't wear," Tod said. "She hardly wore anything. She calls it her punk housewife look. Sleaze in the suburbs."

"Did people laugh?" Charm couldn't help laughing herself.

"They thought it was hilarious!"

"What did she say about you?"

Tod shuddered. It was embarrassing just to think about. He couldn't believe Leonie had been doing that sort of thing all year, using their lives to be funny about in front of all those people. It had been excruciating. It'd made him want to crawl into a corner and hide.

"A lot of stuff about being interested in foxes," he said. "How it was all subli-something."

"Sublimation?"

"Yeah. Jeez, I can't tell you, Charm!" He was going red just thinking about it. He had thought his life was secret and unobserved, but his mother had been watching him all the time—and what she saw was all wrong. She didn't know the real truth—there was no way she could know it. What she had said was twisted and distorted. He was furious with her in a way he had never been before, in a way he would not have thought possible. She had stood up in front of dozens of strangers and made jokes about foxes and sex and puberty, and hearing him howl at the moon like a werewolf, and having to feed him raw meat.

"I hope no one from school was there," Charm said. "What did Dallas and Rick think?"

"Mum didn't make so many jokes about Dallas."

"Dallas is too straight to be funny about," Charm commented.

"She made a few about Grandma though," Tod said. "Just as well she didn't hear them. And Rick nearly killed himself laughing all the way through."

Tod remembered with dislike Rick's booming laugh echoing around the bar, making everyone stare at them more. Rick had been practically crying with laughter. And he'd had his arm around Dallas all night, and afterward, when he'd taken them home, Tod had been sent inside while Rick and Dallas said good night for ages.

He stretched out on the bed and groaned. It had been a terrible day. As soon as he saw Martin at school he remembered he'd been invited to his birthday party on Saturday afternoon. He had completely forgotten about it. On Saturday afternoon the whole family had been at the hospital visiting Charm, and then when he'd got home he had been so exhausted he'd gone straight to bed and slept for about fourteen hours. Martin had pretended nothing had happened. He didn't talk to Tod much, but he didn't mention the missed party so Tod didn't know whether to say anything about it or not. He felt even angrier with his mother when he thought about it. It was all her fault. Other people's mothers kept track of important things like friends' birthday parties and made sure nobody forgot them. Why couldn't Leonie be like that? He felt let down and betrayed by her.

He closed his eyes and saw fox colors swirling behind his lids. His anger made the colors fiercer, and he saw how the first fox picture had had something missing from it. It had been too gentle, too bland. It needed more ferocity and wildness. He ran his tongue over his teeth and felt their hard sharpness.

As though she could read his thoughts Charm said softly, "We've got to go out and do another piece."

"They buffed it, you know," Tod said, without opening his eyes.

"I know. Shaun's really cut up about it. So we're going out again one night this week. Do you want to come?"

"I told him I would."

"Yeah, he said. He was really stoked. It'll be great. That night was such fun. It was the best night of my life. Even worth getting asthma for." She picked up the photo of their father at the trail riding place and studied it, then put it back without saying anything. After a few moments she went on. "Do you think Grandma means it about the police?"

The question made Tod uncomfortable. He didn't want to worry about the legality or not of the painting he was going to do. He couldn't see how it hurt anyone to paint out there along the track in a place which didn't really belong to anyone. And it was none of Grandma's business anyway. True, Shaun had hacked down her plants, but they were so ugly they deserved it. He tried to forget the memory of Grandma so upset she was nearly crying.

"Well, do you?" Charm persisted, picking up an old money box and shaking it.

"I dunno," he said. "She's got a lot tougher lately."

"Yeah, mostly with me. As if getting tough is going to make any difference." The money box hit the floor with a crash.

"When are we going to do the picture?" It made Tod feel good to say *we* like that. He and Charm and Shaun were going to be a team. And they needed him because he could draw and paint.

"One night this week. Shaun'll get you the paints. What colors do you think you'll need?"

Tod wrote out a list for her. Writing the colors down made him quiver with excitement. Red, brown, orange, yellow, ocher—they were just words on paper but they stood for cans and tubes of color which would be translated through him into the most fantastic picture he had ever done.

Before he went to bed that night he tried to get Inkspot into his room, but the old cat had found a cool spot under the water tank and didn't want to move. Tod didn't bother putting pajamas on. He lay down on his bed in his shorts and T-shirt. The room was warm and he slept restlessly, his head full of the picture that was going to come out from inside him and onto the embankment wall. He dreamed of swirling fox colors, of the mysterious animal world, of the strong smells of his fox life and the thrill of hunting and killing. But the rabbit he was chasing in his dream suddenly started to make a horrible noise, like a cat screaming. Tod woke covered in sweat and shaking.

The screaming went on outside for a few more seconds and then was abruptly cut off.

He lay there trying to calm down. He could hear something moving in the yard, the soft pad of paws and a sort of panting.

He got up quietly and went to the back door. Outside he saw two things—Dan Russell, eyes gleaming in the moonlight, foxy muzzle split in a grin. And at his feet a crumpled bundle of fur, black and white.

"Inkspot!" Tod cried. He dropped to his knees and turned the cat over. Its fur was soaked with urine, and there was blood coming out of its mouth. The light had gone out of its eyes.

"Don't be dead," Tod begged. "Inkspot, don't be dead."

Dan Russell snarled softly.

"You killed him," Tod said, turning to look at the big fox. "How could you do that? He never hurt you. Why did you have to kill him?"

Dan Russell fixed Tod with his bright eyes, and the wild feeling leaped between them. Tod found himself trying to resist the swirling change. He was not quite ready for it. He wanted to speak more words, to ask more questions and get answers, but then the feeling grew stronger and stronger and the need for language began to fade.

Cat. Hate. Dan Russell reminded him.

Inkspot . . . Tod couldn't find the pictures in his fox mind for what he wanted to say. Vaguely with his human mind he remembered Inkspot making friends with him, lying on his bed, purring when he stroked him under the chin, but these pictures seemed like something very distant, nothing to do with him, and they faded rapidly away.

He sniffed distastefully at the dead cat, then stretched his legs and sent a long ripple down his spine which made his brush quiver. He felt the strength and suppleness of his fox body. The cat was dead and was no longer of any importance. But he was alive and alert and ready for anything.

Dan Russell looked pleased with himself.

Cat. Dead. Good.

With a swing of his brush, Tod agreed.

Hunting?

Hunting.

Hungry. Tod signaled. Words had disappeared all together. He lifted his muzzle and sniffed the air. Overhead the sky was clear, but toward the southwest the stars had disappeared, swallowed up by a bank of cloud. He could smell rain. But much stronger than the faint smell of rain was the tantalizing, delicious smell of poultry. It made his mouth water and his stomach growl.

Dan Russell had gone very still. His eyes burned brighter and brighter. He was staring intently at the house. Tod saw the foxspell flow out from his eyes. Dan Russell padded down the side of the house and squeezed under the gate. Tod followed him. The foxspell crept in through the windows and under the doors. The two foxes circled the house. Not a sound came from it. Everyone inside was deep asleep. Even the house seemed to have gone to sleep, sinking a little deeper into the earth, giving itself over to the bonds that held it down.

Follow.

Dan Russell leaped effortlessly up the steps. From the chook house came a slight squawk as one of the hens noticed the foxes' shadows gliding up the slope. The drake gave a muffled quack of alarm. Apart from that the night was silent. There was no wind. No bird or cricket made a sound. All Tod could hear was the sound of his and Dan Russell's breathing as they dug under the wire.

Together the two foxes managed it easily. Once they were inside the run the chooks and ducks erupted into a terrified frenzy as the foxes slashed and bit into their soft, feathery bodies. But no human heard them for they were all deep asleep in the fox sleep.

Each fox dragged a dead hen under the wire and carried it back to the quarries. It was hard work climbing the hill, and Tod's neck and jaw muscles were aching by the time they had crawled through the rock tunnel and made their way to Dan Russell's den. There they tore into the carcasses, spitting out the feathers and crunching up the bones. The meat was not as tender as the rabbit, but it tasted sweeter. When they had finished eating they drank from the iron pot, and lay down on the sandy floor of the cave.

Dan Russell sighed in satisfaction.

Tod yawned. He was full and sleepy. It had been good hunting. Wildly exciting with lots to eat at the end. Something worried him at the back of his mind. Something about someone called May. But there was no one called May. The chooks didn't have names, any more than the rabbits did. They were simply things to eat, weak things that didn't have teeth to defend themselves with. He shook his head slightly and blinked his eyes. The worry disappeared and he slept.

He woke once before dawn. In the dim light he could just make out the shape of the big fox, lying on the floor of the cave. Dan Russell's feet twitched as if he were running. He yelped in a high-pitched harsh barking. Tod whimpered. He could feel the nightmare seeping into his skull. The stars were wrong. The land was alien. The earth burnt. There was no way home. He pressed against the sandy floor of the cave, shivering.

When he woke again it was full daylight and Dan Russell, back in his man form, was leaning over him and staring at him.

"Sleep, cub, *yarp*," Dan Russell said. "Daytime now. Stay here and sleep. Tonight we hunt *agai ai ain*."

Tod was about to roll over and do just that, when something came into his mind. Seeing Dan Russell reminded him of the swirling shapes of his dream. Slowly words formed in his mind. He had to do something with the shapes. Paint them. With spray cans. Brushes. He looked down at his paws in surprise. How could he hold anything in them?

Of course, he was a person, not a fox.

Home.

Disappointment flared in Dan Russell's eyes. Reluctantly he let Tod change back. As soon as he was a boy again. Tod leaped to his feet. "It's daytime," he cried. "They'll see I'm not there. They'll be worried about me."

Dan Russell frowned. "Stay with me *snarrul*. It good to have cub *yarp yarp* . . . I make you part of spirit world, and you live here with me *forever ever ever*."

Tod looked at him, remembering the nightmare. He felt

sorry for the fox-man, exiled from his real home, roaming the two worlds, part man and part fox part spirit. He wasn't sure if spirit people could be lonely—but at this moment that was how Dan Russell seemed to him.

"Look *arou ou ound*," Dan Russell whispered. "You see guardians here *yarp*. Stay with me and I make you like them *snarrul*."

Tod looked around the quarry. The sun was not yet high enough to shine into it, but it was filled with clear silvery light. He could see shapes here and there which merged into the rocks and the trees when he looked at them closely. He could see men and women who were both human and animal, like Dan Russell, or human and plant. He recognized the tree spirits, the ash and the olive, and he saw clearly a rabbit-woman and a magpie-man.

There is so much knowledge of the earth here, he thought. He could learn so much and understand so much if he stayed. And it would be the real life of the earth, the one that had lasted for millions of years, not the messy, complicated human world that he was having so much trouble dealing with.

"I teach you many things *yarp*," Dan Russell said. Was that a pleading note in his voice?

"I can't," Tod said. "I'm sorry . . ."

"Sorry!" Dan Russell snarled. "Humans always sorry *snar-rul*. Why do things if *sorry* after?" He turned away from Tod.

"Will I see you again?" Tod asked.

"Call me, I come *yarp yarp*. If not, not," the fox-man snapped.

"Good-bye," Tod said with lowered eyes. With a stab of guilt, he noticed the chicken feathers that lay strewn about the floor of the den. He and Dan Russell had killed Grandma's precious poultry. He wondered if any of them had survived. And

Inkspot—was Inkspot dead or had that been a dream?

No, it was real. Dan Russell had killed Inkspot because he hated cats. While Tod was a fox it hadn't bothered him at all. On the way home he began to remember the things he had forgotten before, and tears sprang in his eyes. Inkspot and the poultry were dead and it was all his fault. He had done those awful things. And he had loved doing it. As he trotted down the hill, stumbling over the rough ground with his bare feet, he recalled the excitement and the thrill of the hunt, and how good the chicken flesh had tasted.

His stomach churned and he thought he was going to be sick. He had no idea what the time was. What if everyone had woken up and found he was gone? What was he going to tell them? No one would ever believe the truth. They'd think he'd gone mad. All he could say was that he'd seen the slaughter in the chook run, and had gone after the foxes. He would never be able to tell anyone it was all his fault.

Tears were pouring down his cheeks now and his breath was coming in deep sobs. He had to wait at the railway for a freight train to go past. 5:47 was its usual time, which meant no one would be awake yet in the house. He ducked under the wire at the top of the yard and went to look at the poultry. He didn't want to see the mess but he forced himself to.

The drake was dead, and so were one of the ducks and the third white leghorn. The two little bantams lay with their heads bitten off. Amazingly the two other ducks had survived. They had bite marks on their necks and chests and one of them trailed a wing. They were glassy eyed and silent with shock. They let Tod examine them. He wondered if they recognized the fox in him. He thought May had disappeared altogether, but she was perched at the top of the run, right under the roof. He was so relieved to see her he started crying all over again.

Inkspot's body was still lying on the concrete path near the water tank. Tod bent down and touched it gently. It was starting to go stiff. Tears dropped from his eyes onto the wet, stained fur. He covered his face with his hands. His fingers smelled of blood.

He wanted someone to comfort him, someone to tell him it would be all right. He ran into the house and into his grandmother's room.

"Grandma," he sobbed, "Grandma, wake up. Something terrible's happened."

She opened her eyes sleepily, stretched, and yawned. When she saw Tod's face she sat bolt upright. "Is it Charm?" she yelled, grabbing Tod by the shoulders.

"No, no," he cried. "It's the foxes. The foxes got in the run and the hens are dead. And Inkspot's dead too."

Grandma gasped a couple of times as if she'd been hit in the stomach. "I'd better come and have a look," she said heavily, getting out of bed, suddenly looking like a tired old woman. She staggered slightly while she was putting on her shoes, and she leaned on Tod for support. Then she pulled him close to her, her arms tight around him.

"Don't cry, love," she said. "Don't upset yourself. These things happen. No one's to blame. No one but the bloody fox."

FOURTEEN

Tod escaped to school as soon as he could. He didn't want to go near the chook run again. He thought Grandma might want his help in burying the dead poultry, but he couldn't stand the thought of it. He felt so guilty it made him angry at his grandmother. She thought he was upset about the fox attack and she'd been really nice to him, gentler than he'd ever known her, but the nicer she was the angrier it made him. He tried to blame her to make himself feel better. It was her fault in a way. She should have had a proper shed for the chooks if she was going to keep them at all. She should have made it impossible for the foxes to get in.

At school Martin was very cool toward him, but he still didn't ask Tod why he hadn't turned up for the birthday party. That made Tod angry too. No wonder the Breakers picked on Martin—he was such a wimp he asked for it. He stayed angry all day. Ms. Linkman added to his rage because he couldn't understand something in math and she kept making him feel more and more stupid. And Adrian mucked around in class, mimicking people with spray cans and mouthing messages at Tod.

He scrawled in Tod's math book, *Shaun says you're in with them.*

I suppose I am, Tod thought. He scribbled back, *Yup!*

Adrian was hyperexcited for the rest of the day. He ended up being kept in after school. Martin retreated from them both, seeking refuge in the resource center.

Tod walked home on his own. He didn't particularly want to go home. He didn't want to see the empty chook run and Grandma's sad face. He walked up the railway line until he came to the concrete slabs on the embankment. The olive green paint was still clean. It would make a good background, he thought. A good background for the foxes.

He climbed up the steep side of the cutting, and sat halfway up the hill looking out over the suburbs toward the sea. From time to time he picked out a stone from the shaley ground and lobbed it across the train track. He thought back to the time he'd sat on the hillside with Grandma in the yard, waiting for the fox. It seemed like a lifetime ago. That kid had been just a child who didn't know anything. He sat there, throwing stones and feeling angry until hunger drove him home.

Seeing Rick's car parked in the street outside the house didn't improve his mood. He went to his room, and tried not to think about Inkspot. He had homework, but there was no point looking at it, as he wasn't going to understand it anyway. He stuck the picture of Laurie up on the wall with a piece of blue tack, and threw his old compasses at it, like a dart.

Dallas came to tell him tea was ready.

"Hey, you've made a bit of a mess of the wall," she said. "What's up?"

When Tod just shrugged without replying she said, "You must be really upset about the chooks. Isn't it a shame? Foxes are awful animals. They should all be wiped out, that's what I think."

"You don't know anything," he burst out. "You think you're so smart, but you don't know anything!"

"I know a darn sight more than you ever will," she snapped back, and instantly looked horrified. "Sorry, Toddy, I shouldn't have said that!"

"It's what you think, though, isn't it? It's what you all think. That I'm really dumb?"

"Of course we don't think that," she said, too quickly for him to believe her. "Don't worry about it. Soon as my exams are over, I'll be able to give you some tutoring—help you catch up before high school, hey?" She came into the room and tried to pat him on the shoulder. He shrugged her off, backing away. He knew he'd hurt her feelings, but he couldn't bear to be mothered by her anymore.

"Come and eat," she said shortly and left the room. After a few moments Tod followed her. He didn't want to talk to anyone, but he was hungry.

Grandma was standing at the stove serving out the meal. It seemed to be a sort of stew, with a wonderful meaty smell. Tod's mouth began to water and his stomach growled.

"Someone's hungry," Grandma remarked.

"I think he's grown an inch since yesterday," Rick said. He was leaning against the sink. He reached out and pulled Tod toward him. "Come here, tiger!" He tried to measure Tod up against himself, but Tod wriggled away. How come everyone was so keen to touch him? Why didn't they leave him alone?

"Tod," Dallas said, "Rick's only trying to be friendly!"

She and Rick exchanged a look over Tod's head, a look that said, *he'll come around, he's just being a silly kid.* Tod sat down at the table so violently the cutlery rattled and the glasses shook.

"What's wrong with you, Tod?" his mother asked. She had

rings under her eyes and looked tired.

"It hasn't been a very good day," he said.

"Never mind, love, you'll get over it. Life's full of these ups and downs." Leonie looked around the room. "At least, that's half right! Does anyone know where Charm is?"

"Wouldn't have a clue," Dallas said. "Come on, Rick, sit down and eat." She touched him on the shoulder and he smiled at her as though no one else in the room existed.

Tod noticed but his mother was oblivious. "Do you know where Charm is, Tod?"

"Probably out somewhere with Shaun." He wondered if they were getting the paints, and when they would come and get him. He was aware of Rick's eyes on him and tried to look unconcerned.

Grandma finished serving and sat down herself, sighing heavily. "I'm surprised you let her go out with him," she grumbled to Leonie. "I'd put a stop to it, if she were my daughter."

"He's a good source of material, isn't he, Mum?" Dallas said.

"It's not something to joke about," Grandma snapped. " 'My daughter's boyfriend, the vandal and graffiti artist.' Kids like that waste their own lives and ruin everyone else's. You should do something about it before she goes off the tracks altogether."

"Charm's not going to go off the tracks," Leonie said. "But she's got to work things out for herself. I'm not going to run her life for her."

"You'll wish you had when she gets pregnant," Grandma said. "Or ends up a drug addict."

"She's not going to be a drug addict," Leonie said. She was starting to sound irritated. "Lots of kids experiment with drugs and don't become addicts. And she knows all about contraception, and safe sex and all that."

"But some kids experiment and don't come out of it safely, Mrs. Crofton," Rick put in.

"My name is Leonie," she told him. "And if you can't bring yourself to use it, then call me Ms. Crofton."

He grinned at her, quite unsnubbed. "Right you are, Ms. Leonie Crofton." She gave him a black look. She didn't really like Rick, Tod realized, even though he'd laughed so much at her act. Perhaps he'd laughed too much.

"I don't understand why the police don't do something about kids like Shaun Stone," Grandma went on. "You know who he is, what he's up to. Why don't you arrest him?"

"We don't like arresting kids," Rick replied. "Nine times out of ten, anyway, a good talking to is all they need. Shaun's a tougher nut than most, I agree, but we try to keep kids out of the courts. Frankly, it's not proving very productive for anyone the way the law works. And if someone like Shaun gets sent to a remand center, chances are he'll come out worse than he went in." Rick took a mouthful of stew and said, still chewing, "We're keeping an eye on young Shaun, though. I guess you could say he's on his last chance."

Rick sounded so pompous, Tod thought. He looked at his mother and guessed from the way her mouth tightened that she thought so too.

He'd eaten his stew almost without noticing it. "Is there any more?" he asked.

"Help yourself, Tod," Grandma told him. "This is delicious, Dallas. You're going to make someone a good wife."

Tod knew this was the sort of comment his mother hated, like "boys will be boys." He looked at her again as he got up to see if she was going to respond, but before Leonie could say anything, Rick remarked, "Yes, she will. Me."

There was a moment's silence, as if everyone were waiting for Dallas to speak up and deny it, but she said nothing, just sat and smiled almost pleadingly. Rick reached over and took her hand. Her face went bright red, and she had to look down.

"This is a joke," Leonie said.

"No," Rick replied. "I've asked Dallas to marry me."

"When I've finished my exams," Dallas managed to say, with a gulp.

"Are you out of your mind?" Leonie yelled. "You're only seventeen! What would you want to get married for?"

"I told you she'd hate it," Dallas said to Rick.

"We love each other, Mrs. Crofton," Rick said. "When people love each other they get married."

"Don't call me Mrs.," Leonie shrieked. She pushed her plate away from her roughly. "Dallas is not 'people.' She's my daughter. She's extremely intelligent. She's going to have a career. She doesn't want to be held back by being married, especially not to someone in the police."

"I'm still going to have a career," Dallas said. "I'm going to do everything the same, except I'm going to be married to Rick and living with him while I do it, and it'll all be much easier, because I won't have to be looking after Charm and Tod and you while I do it. You'll all have to look after yourselves!"

"I'll never understand you, Leonie," Grandma said. "You're making the kind of fuss about Dallas getting married that you should be making about Charmian."

"You can't talk," Leonie retorted, turning in fury on her mother. "You made exactly the same sort of scene here in this kitchen, when Laurie and I told you we were getting married."

Tod was starting to feel very uncomfortable. The row around him was making him shake, but he felt as if he was frozen to the floor and couldn't get away. When Leonie was in a rage she said awful things, things she was sorry about afterward and claimed she didn't mean, but it was too late then because she'd said them, and the words were still there.

"You and Laurie had a damn sight less sense than these two," Grandma said. "At least Dallas can cook, and Rick's got a job and a future!"

"You can't stop us, Mum," Dallas said. There were tears in her eyes, but she sounded determined.

"I most certainly can," Leonie yelled. "You're underage for a start. I'll never give my consent."

"What happened to not trying to run people's lives?" Dallas was starting to yell now too. "You won't interfere in Charm's life, but you're quite happy to try and ruin mine."

"I'm trying to stop you ruining your life." Leonie's voice was getting higher and higher. "Getting married at seventeen is the most stupid thing I've ever heard."

She was taking a breath to say more when the phone rang shrilly. No one moved.

"Could someone answer that?" Leonie said icily. "Tod, go and get it. If it's for me say I'll call them back."

Having something to do meant Tod could unfreeze from where he was still standing by the stove. He put his plate in the sink. He wasn't hungry anymore anyway. He thought the phone would stop before he could reach it, but it rang on and on as he went down the passageway.

When he lifted up the receiver he could hear a sort of distant echoing noise.

"Hello," he said, and heard his own voice echo back to him faintly.

"Hello, Tod?" He would have known the voice anywhere, even distorted as it was now. "Is that you, Tod?"

"Dad?" he said, not quite believing that it really could be

his father. Then both of them said, "How are you?" at the same time.

To his astonishment, Tod felt his face begin to work uncontrollably. He listened to Laurie's voice, unable to say anything.

"I got your letter, mate. And the picture. The picture's really terrific. I love it. So how's everything? Can't wait to see you."

Tod made a huge effort and got his voice back. He could hear Leonie yelling in the kitchen. And it sounded as if Dallas was crying. Even Rick had raised his voice to try to get Leonie to listen to him.

"Dad? I think you should come home! Are you coming home soon?"

"Yes, I am! It was in the letter that got lost! I'll be home before Christmas. What's all that noise in the background, Tod? What's going on?"

"Dad, Dallas wants to get married and Mum's furious."

There was another echoing silence from the other end of the phone line. Tod thought the line had gone dead, but then his father spoke again. "I'd better talk to Mum. Get her for me, would you, Tod. Bye, mate."

He laid the receiver carefully on the hall table and went back to the kitchen. Leonie was in full spate. Dallas was crying and Grandma had started clearing the table with quick, angry movements.

"Mum," Tod began.

"I told you I'd call them back!"

"Mum, it's Dad! He's phoning from England."

Immediately he'd said it he realized it was a mistake. It made Leonie even angrier. She swore, and pushed her chair back from the table violently. Dallas jumped up too.

"I want to talk to him!"

Leonie was shaking with rage when she picked up the phone. Tod could feel it flowing out from her as he listened in the passage. She was holding Dallas off with one hand as Dallas clamored, "Let me talk to him! I want to talk to him!"

Leonie shouted furiously, "It's no good, Laurie. You can't just swan off for six months and expect to come back and find us all the same. . . . I like being on my own. . . . Home for Christmas? That's just the sort of sentimental rubbish I thought you were going away to sort out. . . . You can't come back!"

She's angry, Tod told himself as he crept silently back to his own room. She doesn't mean it. He threw himself on the bed and buried his head in his pillow. It's not true. He's going to come back anyway. She can't make him stay away. We're his family too and if he wants to come back he can.

He heard yelling from the kitchen and then the house shook as a door slammed. There was silence for a little while. Tod lay in a curious half-awake state. He was no longer crying. His feelings seemed to have gone underground completely. The water pipes banged in the laundry. Someone must be washing up, Grandma probably, practicing her shock therapy.

About a quarter of an hour later, he heard footsteps outside and the door to his room opened.

"You all right, love?" Grandma said.

He was angry that she hadn't thought to knock. He didn't say anything. Grandma came in anyway and sat on the end of the bed. "Don't worry about the barney. Everyone says things they don't mean sometimes. Your mother'll calm down, they'll sort things out."

But it was Grandma who had said, all those months ago, that Laurie had run out on them. So she wasn't really being truthful now, she was just saying it to make him feel better.

It made him feel worse, because Grandma still thought he was the little boy who could be comforted with fairy stories. She touched him on the shoulder, and he longed to turn over and throw himself into her arms—but he couldn't because he wasn't what Grandma thought he was. He lay without saying anything, without even raising his head from the pillow. After a few moments she sighed, patted him on the shoulder, got off the bed, and left the room, closing the door behind her.

Tod turned over onto his back. The light faded slowly as he waited.

FIFTEEN

Tod must have fallen asleep, for suddenly he was dreaming. In his dream he was taking his father to see something along the railway track. He had a sense of panic, as if he was going to be too late for whatever it was they were going to see, but Dad refused to hurry. He kept stopping on the track, in the middle of the rails, to look at things. . . .

Then just as suddenly he was awake, and Charm was shaking him soundlessly.

"Come on," she mouthed at him. "We're going now."

Tod pushed the sheet back and swung his legs out of bed. He followed his sister to the back door. It creaked loudly as she unlocked it, and they both froze, but no sound came from the house. Outside he stopped to put on his sneakers. The night was mild, and the gully wind was blowing strongly. The moon gave a little light. The traffic noise had stilled. He wondered how many hours there would be before dawn. As they went out the front gate and crossed the road to walk to the reserve, they could see all the lights of the suburbs, orange and white, stretching away to the coastline.

"Pretty," Charm whispered.

Tod nodded, but there was something about the lights that made him uneasy. They shouldn't really be there. The whole land should be dark at night, like the bush on the other side of the depot. He turned his eyes to the blackness there. It was restful. It had always been like that at night. If you could see the whole history of the land speeded up, the lights before them would appear like a tiny flicker right at the end, something you would think you had only imagined. During all the other unimaginable number of nights the land before them would have been dark.

He shook his head. He and Charm cut across the reserve to the creek. Then they moved up toward the railway line in the cover of the trees and shrubs. Tod padded silently, all senses alert, but behind him Charm made much more noise, slipping and stumbling, swearing when she stumbled, and then giggling.

Shaun was waiting for them by the grave of the dead fox. There was hardly any smell left from it now. It had returned completely to the earth. Shaun, though, smelled quite strongly of the usual cigarette smoke, sweat, and a nervousness that Tod noticed immediately.

"Hey," he greeted them quietly, pulling Charm toward him with a possessive gesture that both surprised and irritated Tod. Tod himself took a step back. He didn't want anyone touching him. He thought Shaun might say something special to him, but Shaun seemed preoccupied. They headed toward the storm-water drain in silence.

Shaun's nervousness made Tod even more wary. He swung his head from side to side, sniffing the night air. Below the normal nighttime smells, he caught a whiff of something else.

Humans.

He stopped abruptly. "Someone's in the drain," he whispered.

"Yeah, it's okay. It's Justin and the others."

"What are they doing here?"

"New development," Shaun said, ducking into the drain. "Come on."

Tod followed him. His teeth were clenched and the hair on the back of his neck was prickling. He didn't like going down into the dark space. It felt like walking into a trap. But Charm was coming along behind him, muttering when she scraped her head on the roof. The Breakers wouldn't hurt him while she was there. And he was one of them now, wasn't he? Adrian had written it down in his math book. *Shaun says you're in with them.* He was. And he was going to do the piece for Shaun to prove it.

All the same his senses were on edge as he approached the group at the far end of the drain. Adrenaline pumped through his body, making his joints tingle. The boys' shapes were silhouetted against the tunnel opening, slightly darker than the night world beyond. He couldn't see them well enough to be sure who was there, but he thought there were four of them—which meant Justin and Dom and probably the two younger boys who'd been on the train, Jamie and Luke.

He wondered why they were there. Surely they weren't all going to watch him paint. Perhaps they were going to be lookouts. But he could feel their nervous excitement. Something was up.

"Wait here," Shaun said quietly. Tod squatted down while the older boy went ahead. He could hear the gang whispering, but he couldn't quite catch what they were saying.

"Yuck!" Charm sat down next to him. "I hope there's nothing gross here."

"Sshh!" Tod muttered. His head was down and his ears straining.

The boys seemed to be arguing. Their voices grew more heated and louder. Justin in particular sounded angry and insistent. In contrast Shaun seemed almost conciliatory.

"Do you know what's going on?" Tod whispered to Charm.

"Justin's getting restless," she said, making no attempt to lower her voice. "He thinks Shaun's losing his grip. He doesn't think they have enough action."

"Are they going to paint too?"

"Just some tags here and there, probably. They don't go for the big paintings like Shaun. They think it's a waste of time. It's only going to get buffed. And you're too likely to get caught before you've finished."

"Am I?"

"No, not you, necessarily. Anyone. You'll have lookouts. You should be okay."

Tod felt the adrenaline surge again.

"If it's not dangerous, it's no fun," Charm added.

The argument at the mouth of the drain came to an end. "Okay, okay," Shaun was saying. "Do it your way."

"We're going to," Justin said, loud enough for Tod and Charm to hear him clearly. "Let's get moving."

Shaun came back to Charm and Tod, moving fast, although he had to bend double.

"Come on," he said.

"What's going on?" Charm asked. "Ouch, my leg's gone to sleep."

"Justin's got something to do at the depot. Well, it's okay. If anything it'll create a diversion for us." Shaun's voice was high-pitched and tense. "But we'd better get going before they start. They're going to set off the alarms for sure, so we need to be down the track before then."

"You're not chickening out?" Justin's voice came out of the darkness.

"I've got something of my own to do tonight," Shaun replied shortly.

"Bull! You're not going to be doing anything. Just watching while the kid plays with paints. We always said we'd do the depot. You said you'd be in it!"

"Okay, okay. I'll be in it!" Shaun gave Tod a little shove. "You get started. Here, the paints are in the bag. Charm's got the flashlight. She'll be your lookout."

"We need two," Charm put in.

"Adrian, you there?"

The smallest shape, the one Tod had assumed was Luke, came toward them.

"Here, boss!" Adrian said smartly, making a salute and yelping as he hit his hand on the drain wall.

"Adrian?" Tod said. "What are you doing here?"

"I'm in too, aren't I, Shaun?"

"If you behave yourself and do what you're told," Shaun hissed.

"Come on, come on," Justin said. "It's going to be daylight before we've started."

"Give them a chance to get there," Shaun said. He tried to make it sound like an order, but it came out as a plea. Justin made a noise of irritation and contempt.

Tod took the bag and squeezed past the boys to get out of the drain. He could feel their excitement, smell their fear. They were about to explode again as they had on the train. He had a moment of doubt. Something terrible was going to happen. He should go home now. He didn't want to be part of it. . . .

But he'd told Shaun he'd do the painting. And even if he hadn't made that promise, he still had to do it for his own sake. It had to get out from inside his head. Anyway, he would be along the track. Nothing to do with whatever was going to happen at the depot.

"I'll be up there soon." Shaun kissed Charm on the lips

outside the drain entrance. Someone whistled, the noise echoing through the tunnel.

"Get stuffed," Charm shouted back at whoever it was. Then she followed Tod and Adrian up the steep track.

Tod was panting by the time they reached the top of the cutting. The bag was heavy on his shoulder. They stopped and took long deep breaths. The moon was over the sea, casting a reflection like a silver road.

"Is this where you're going to do it?" Adrian asked, looking down.

"This is where Shaun and I did his," Charm said. "Hope yours lasts a bit longer, Toddy."

Looking at the blank wall of the cutting made Tod's heart race again. Without saying anything he started climbing down the steep slope. It was dangerously slippery. Several times he slid a yard or two, before grabbing hold of a plant or bush. Finally he went backward, on hands and knees, until he made it to the top of the concrete slab where there was just room for him to perch. He took the bag off his back and placed it on the bank, hooking the strap around a tree root.

He was about three yards above the ground. If he climbed down to ground level he wouldn't be able to reach up very far. If he stayed where he was he would have to do the painting upside down, but it would be where he wanted it, at the top of the slab.

"Hey, where do we go?" Adrian yelled. "Do we come down there with you?"

"Shout a bit louder, Adrian," Charm said sarcastically. "They might have missed that in Redwood."

"Aw, no one's out here!" Adrian began climbing down the slope. Halfway down he began to slide. He made a couple of futile grabs at the ground, but couldn't stop his fall, until he got to where Tod was. They teetered together on the top of the slab, just managing to keep their balance. Adrian sat down heavily. Tod fell on top of him.

"Stop fooling around," Charm hissed. Adrian was making her nervous, and Tod began to catch the nervousness from her.

"Adrian, get down by the track and watch from there," he told him, and helped him climb down. "Charm, stay where you are. If anyone does come up the railway track you can get away quicker from there."

"I'm about to fall off altogether," Charm complained, sliding a few more feet as she spoke. She made a frantic grab at a kangaroo thorn bush. "Hell! More thorns! It was a damn sight easier last time, I'm telling you. I stayed down below and Shaun did the acrobatics." She settled herself down, anchoring her feet against the spindly trunk of the kangaroo thorn. "Okay, maestro. You can begin."

Working on the top of the slab was painfully hard. Several times Tod nearly overbalanced and the fear of falling made him slow. He kept getting terrible cramps in his legs and arms from the strange positions he had to take up, so he could only work for a few minutes at a time before he had to stand and stretch. The moonlight, which had seemed so bright when they were walking through the bush, gave the wrong sort of light for painting. He couldn't see the colors properly, and the outlines wobbled and faded. When he stopped to stretch he used the flashlight to check on how the painting looked, but after a while the battery started to fade.

He drew the outlines first with the thick black magic marker, lying on his stomach to reach down as far as he could. The foxes ran along the top of the greenish concrete, their legs and brushes intertwined and fluid. They twisted in and out of the trunks of trees and bushes, and under their feet Tod drew the rocky ground, grasses and flowers, the water of the creek, the deep drinking holes.

Then he added the colors, mainly reds, oranges, and browns, fox colors and earth colors, in the swirls and shapes that had filled his dreams for so long.

He worked without consciously thinking about what he was doing, as though his fingers knew instinctively what to paint next. Into his emptied mind came images and memories that his hands translated into the picture without his brain interfering at all.

He remembered the wild feeling that leaped into his eyes from Dan Russell, the energy that rushed into his paws from the earth when he was a fox, his animal alertness and physical joy. He remembered the perseverance and stamina of the fox, the cunning and strength that made it outlast its enemies. He drew on the fox feeling to keep on painting, even when his arms ached with the strain and he was dizzy with fatigue.

He saw the tree spirits and felt their powerful presence all around him. He remembered the rabbit-woman, the taste of the freshly killed rabbit in his mouth, the fierceness of the wild cat, his own pitiless ferocity when he'd killed the chooks, the death of Inkspot, and his grief.

The fox feeling and his human self were all mixed up in the picture. Everything that had happened to him since he'd come to live at his grandmother's was in it—sorrow and excitement, pain and fear, pity and rage, living and dying.

Charm, from her perch on the hillside, kept herself awake by singing all her favorite rock songs. There would be long periods of silence, in which Tod thought she had fallen asleep, and then she would suddenly start up again, making him jump, then smile.

Adrian sat on the other side of the railway line for a while, but then he got bored and came back to talk to Tod.

"Isn't this cool?" he said. "Aren't you glad we're in with them now?"

Tod was concentrating hard and didn't answer.

"Bet Martin wouldn't ever dare do this," Adrian said with a note of scorn. "This beats playing his dumb old computer game, doesn't it?"

Tod felt a twinge of guilt thinking about Martin. He added an angry twist to the fox's mouth. If only Martin wasn't so cautious about everything.

"What happened to Luke?" he asked Adrian.

"Got busted nicking paints. His parents went ape. Justin's afraid he'll tell them everyone's names. That's why he's so tense tonight." Adrian sat down at the base of the slab, leaned his back against it, and yawned. Tod thought he'd fallen asleep too, but after a while he said, "It's a bit spooky here. Do you reckon this place is haunted?"

Tod thought of the spirit world, whose fringes he'd touched, and which he knew lay all around them, just on the edge of their own reality. But he knew that wasn't what Adrian meant.

"No ghosts," he said.

"Lots of people must have died here though," Adrian persisted. "When the quarries were working, and they were putting in the railway. There'd have been accidents and fights and murders." His voice was becoming more and more melodramatic, and though Tod couldn't see his face he guessed Adrian had assumed one of his looks. Horror, probably, or terror. Adrian went on talking and Tod half listened. He didn't want to have to talk—it was too distracting, but Adrian didn't seem to mind. He talked on and Tod went on painting.

His arms were aching and his eyes were itchy and sore by the time the moon had disappeared into the sea. It was the darkest time of the night. He could hardly see to paint at all. Adrian had said nothing for a while and Charm had also been quiet for a long time. Good lookouts, Tod grumbled to himself. They're both asleep!

He stood up and stretched his arms over his head, took a deep breath, and shook his head from side to side to loosen the muscles in his neck. Something caught his attention. The night had been quiet and peaceful a few moments before but now something was wrong—a strange noise—he could only just hear it but he was aware of it disturbing the web of normal nighttime sounds.

He listened intently. In the silence a magpie sang abruptly, echoed by another and another. But behind the waking birds there was something else, a vague, disembodied voice that came in snatches from the direction of the depot.

You have violated . . . area . . . were called . . . immediately . . . protected . . . police . . . leave . . .

"Charm, Adrian," he shouted. "Listen. It's the alarm at the depot."

"We'd better leave," Charm yelled back.

"I've nearly finished. I'll only be a few more minutes." He crouched down again, leaning over the edge of the slab, forcing his tired hands to go more quickly. He had just one corner to fill in. He realized he could almost see the colors again. It was nearly dawn. The painting was emerging slowly as the sky brightened.

Tod breathed out deeply. The picture was all right. It

looked like it had looked inside his head—not completely, but close enough. Yes, definitely close enough. He stood up painfully, working his fingers backward and forward to get the cramps out.

"Tod!" Charm was calling. He caught a note of alarm in her voice and looked up.

"They've really hit the depot," she shouted. "I think it's on fire!"

As she spoke there came a muffled explosion, followed by another, louder one. The sky lit up. They could see black smoke rising slowly above the edge of the hillside.

"Shit!" Tod muttered, packing up the paints as quickly as he could. "We'd better get out of here. Adrian, get moving!"

"Give me a hand," Adrian said. "I'll never get back up on my own."

"Run along the track," Tod told him. "It's easier to climb up near the tunnel. We'll meet you at the top."

His heart was racing and all tiredness had disappeared. He hadn't really thought about what would happen when they'd finished the picture. It had been like a game. But if the depot was on fire, and the police were on their way . . .

"Hurry up!" Charm yelled. Her voice sounded as if she were thinking the same sort of thing.

Tod was scrambling up the slope when he heard way down the track a distant hoot. It was the early morning freight on its way through to Melbourne.

"Adrian," he shrieked. "Get off the track before the train comes." He was turning back, thinking he should help pull Adrian up the side of the cutting when his quick hearing caught something else. He could hear running footsteps, heavy breathing. He was stuck, fully visible, on the side of the hill. Stupidly he tried to hide the bag of paints behind his back.

Shaun came around the corner. His face was drawn with excitement and fear. He waved briefly at Tod as he took in the painting. "It's cool," he yelled. "Wow, is it cool!"

"What's happening back there?" Tod shouted.

"Place is a madhouse," Shaun said, laughing, and then almost sobbing. "Justin and Jamie went berserk. I've got to get out of here. There are cops everywhere. I'll do time for this one, if they get me. I'm out of here."

Another dull explosion and a crackle of fire made him look back briefly down the track.

"It's all burning," he said. "Beautiful! You should have been there, babe," he yelled up at Charm. "It was a great night."

The noise of the train grew louder. It was nearly at the bend. They could hear it slowing as the gradient steepened.

"Gotta catch my train," Shaun said cheerfully. "I'll see you around."

"Shaun," Charm shrieked from the hillside. "You can't just go!"

"I can't stay either!" he shouted. "I'll be back for you, Charm. I promise. I'll come back for you."

The train rounded the corner. The driver must have seen them, for the whistle sounded, long and piercing. Shaun gave a half wave and began to run alongside the flatbeds.

"Be careful!" Charm was scrambling back down the hill as if she could physically stop Shaun from going.

The train must have been moving faster than it looked. Shaun had to speed up to keep up with it. It wasn't like in the old movies, Tod realized, when it looked quite easy to swing yourself into a boxcar. The flatbeds, laden with containers, didn't offer much space either to get yourself on, or to sit once you were on.

Charm shouted, "He's going to kill himself."

Shaun made a leap for the coupling, grabbed on to a rail, and swung himself up. For a moment he balanced on the edge of the flatbed. His hands scrabbled trying to get a grip. The train lurched to one side, throwing him up against the container. He found a handhold, and quickly pulled himself around to the back of the flatbed where there was just space to crouch. He waved and grinned.

"Shaun!" Just before the tunnel, Adrian caught sight of his brother. "Shaun! Don't leave me here!"

"Adrian," Shaun shouted. "Don't! Don't try it!"

"I'm coming with you."

Tod caught sight of Adrian's face. Its look was set and determined. Not assumed. Real.

It all happened very quickly. One moment Adrian was in the air, alive and full of purpose, then, as Tod and Charm both screamed together, he slipped between the couplings and fell under the train.

ENDING

From the bush above the railway tunnel, the big fox heard a scream. He listened intently. Something cried again, a sharp piercing sound like a fatally wounded animal.

Human cub.

Calling.

Dan Russell left the bone he had been crunching up and trotted off in the direction of the scream.

Below his feet he felt the faint vibration of the earth as the freight train passed through the tunnel. All around him birds were celebrating the new day. Soon the sun would be up; he should be heading for his den in the quarry, but the human cub had called him again.

He lifted his nose. There was a strange smell on the cool morning air, a heavy choking smell that made his hackles rise.

Fire.

He hesitated. He heard the cry again, less piercing now but more insistent. He heard other more distant noises too, the wailing of sirens, the roar of engines.

Danger.

The human cub was in danger. He must go and help him.

The decision taken, Dan Russell leaped down the slope. At the top of the cutting he stopped and stared down. He did not see the fox picture at his feet, even though it looked like his own reflection. He saw his human cub by the train track, bending over something that did not move. He could smell blood.

Death.

His human was making strange sounds, no longer screaming but panting in a heavy anguished way that made Dan Russell want to snarl and run. He wanted to save his cub. He wanted to take him away from whatever it was that made him pant like that. He barked sharply. Then he waited for his cub to look up and meet his gaze.